THE NIGHT OF THE WOLF

THE NIGHT OF THE WOLF

Paul Halter

Translated by Robert Adey and John Pugmire

WILDSIDE PRESS

THE NIGHT OF THE WOLF

———

First published in French in 2000 by
Editions du Masque – Hachette Livre as *La Nuit du Loup.*

THE NIGHT OF THE WOLF. Copyright © Editions du Masque, 2000.
English translation copyright © by John Pugmire 2004.

Of the translated stories that comprise this collection two have previously been published in *Ellery Queen's Mystery Magazine* : "The Tunnel of Death" in the March / April 2005 issue; "The Night of the Wolf," in a slightly modified form, in the May 2006 issue; and in addition the same magazine featured in its July 2004 issue a different translation (by Peter Schulman) of "The Call of the Lorelei."

For information, please contact Wildside Press at
9710 Traville Gateway Dr #234, Rockville, MD, 20850-7408.

FIRST AMERICAN EDITION: November 2006

Library of Congress Cataloging-in-Publication Data
Halter, Paul
[*Nuit du Loup*. English]
The Night of the Wolf: a collection of short stories / Paul Halter;
translated from the French by Robert Adey and John Pugmire

To our wives, Helen and Sue,
for their encouragement, help and tolerant understanding

TABLE OF CONTENTS

—

FOREWORD

___

Robert Adey

Funny how time slips by. And difficult to believe that it's almost fifty years since I read my first locked room mystery. It was one of John Dickson Carr's and, in stumbling, as I did, across this particular author, I must count myself extremely fortunate because, in terms of impossible crimes, locked room murders and other fictional detective mysteries in which the seemingly inexplicable is made abundantly and logically clear, Carr was the undisputed maestro.

His books inevitably led me on to other authors, Victorian and Edwardian, golden age and contemporary (by which I mean pretty well anything written after 1950) who had tried their hands at the same sort of impossible puzzle. For most of them it was just a book or two in this vein, some of them reasonably good, others decidedly not. But there were a few authors who, like Carr, tended to make a speciality of impossible crime novels and short stories. There weren't many of them to be sure, and the results in some cases were pretty awful: lamentable prose; prolix, sometimes impenetrable plotting and solutions that didn't so much creak like an old gate, but actually fell off the hinges. However among them there were also a handful who managed to produce works that combined both clever plotting and good writing—something which by and large Carr had done throughout his working life almost, it appeared, without effort, and certainly with remarkably few failures.

So it was that I next immersed myself in the stories of these successful, if generally less prolific, impossible crime specialists, writers such as Clayton Rawson, Hake Talbot, Joseph Commings, Arthur Porges and John Sladek and, of those still alive and most definitely kicking, Ed Hoch and Bill Pronzini.

Over the years I have read more tales of impossible crime than I care to remember and the day inevitably arrived when the palate had become decidedly jaded, and only a very exceptional tale was really able to engage my interest.

It was therefore with no particular expectations that, a few years ago, I was first introduced to the works of Frenchman, Paul Halter. Friends from across the English Channel had spoken in glowing terms of this young writer's artistry as a novelist in the field of impossible crime, but, because my ability to read French was still grounded at basic schoolboy level, it was not until one of his novels was translated into English for me that I was able to sample the wares myself. Right away I realised that here was the work of a true genius in the art of constructing and solving miraculous crimes, and I was delighted later on to have the privilege of playing a small part in producing a translation of the stories in the present collection—which incidentally represent just a tiny fraction of Paul's output during the last twenty years.

Make no mistake about it. The tales you are about to read are no ordinary run of the mill yarns of murder and mystery. As impossible crime stories they are absolutely the finished article, packed with the sort of original invention, ingenuity and downright cunning that Carr produced in his golden years. Add to this a distinctly Gallic flair for dramatic setting and characterisation and you have before you one of the biggest treats in years for the student of miracle murders.

Carr himself spent time in Paris and was a fervent admirer of French detective fiction; the influence of such French writers as Gaston Leroux is not difficult to spot in Carr's own books and the American maestro's first series detective, Henri Bencolin, was of course himself a Frenchman.

So it seems to me singularly appropriate that this modern day disciple of John Dickson Carr is French. The wheel has perhaps come full circle.

—Robert Adey

INTRODUCTION

Roland Lacourbe

"Truth, I may remind you, is stranger than fiction."

"Spare me that tedious lie. You are quoting the only paradox which un-imaginative people ever succeeded in inventing. And it is not true. It is in-sidious propaganda on the part of cheerless souls who want to make fiction as dull as truth . . . What we need is some fearless iconoclast who will come out boldly against this damnable tyranny, saying, 'Fiction is stranger than truth.'"

Henri Bencolin *The Lost Gallows*

Starting from this premise, spoken by one of John Dickson Carr's favourite characters, certain authors blessed with a vivid imagination have been tempted to raise the stakes by basing their stories on the most notoriously strange occurrences. Paul Halter is such an author, and this first collection of his short stories was inspired to a large extent by real events as weird as the strangest fiction.

The giant escalator which forms the backdrop for the murders in *The Tunnel of Death* is based on the very real escalator 'Montmorency' inaugurated in 1928 in Le Havre. One hundred and seventy-six meters long and rising fifty meters during the ascent, it was the biggest in Europe at the time and could carry five thousand people during its peak hour. Although classified a historic monument, it was closed to the public in 1984 for economic reasons. Asked to write a story set in these unusual surroundings (with the usual proviso of 'all resemblance to persons living or dead, etc., etc.'), Paul Halter has risen to the occasion: creating a seemingly impossible situation, but one where all the clues are planted in the text with scrupulous fairness.

Sealed crypts whose apertures have remained undisturbed for years, yet inside which coffins have been found in complete disarray: the restless cemetery in Stanton, Suffolk, in 1755; the creeping coffins of Barbados in 1820; the unquiet graves of Oesel in the Baltic in 1844, are just a few of the unusual but rigorously documented occurrences. In telling the extraordinary tale of the displaced coffins in David Simmons' family vault in his superbly macabre story *The Dead Dance at Night*, Paul Halter evokes the celebrated *The Burning Court* and *The Sleeping Sphinx* of John Dickson Carr, his inspiration and to whom, over the last twenty years, he has proved to be a truly worthy successor.

There are other examples of reality twisted and falsified, yet at the same time elaborated and enriched: the myths and legends of folklore. Heinrich Heine's celebrated adaptation of the German tale of the Lorelei, a siren luring vessels on to the fatal rocks by her beautiful and irresistible singing, must surely have its origins in the Naiads of Hellenic myth and tales of real shipwrecks past. Paul Halter uses the Lorelei legend as the foundation of one of his most haunting stories, *The Call of the Lorelei*, set in his native Alsace. More terrifying altogether is the legend of the werewolf, whose origins are lost in time but which nevertheless must again have been based on some past incident whose causes were unknown or forgotten, such as the trials of Gilles Garnier of Dole in 1573 and Peter Stubbe of Cologne in 1591, which are a matter of historical record. In the brilliant and exotic *The Night of the Wolf*, he weaves a tale of werewolves, all the more unnerving because it avoids the usual anthropomorphism.

Obviously, true to his obsessions and fantasies, Paul Halter devotes most of his time to his favourite theme, namely that of the 'locked-room' which is featured in eight of the nine stories* contained in this book, running the gamut of variations possible. In the classic *Murder in Cognac*, a reclusive writer has taken refuge at the top of a guarded tower as a result of death threats, but all to no avail. In the macabre and ghostly *The Abominable Snowman*, a homicidal snowman is seen by a terrified witness slashing its victim to death. And in the paranormal *The Cleaver*, a gruesome murder is foreseen in a premonitory dream in one of Paul Halter's most extraordinary and accomplished stories, which I have no hesitation in declaring to be a masterpiece of crime fiction.

A ghostly and elusive criminal who terrorizes London and commits unspeakable atrocities while killing prostitutes; a mad killer whose identity and motives will forever remain shrouded in mystery; whose name will live in eternal infamy as Jack the Ripper: this baffling enigma inspired *Rippermania*, the name of a curious malady which afflicts certain eccentrics who exhibit a morbid curiosity with the most hideous crimes of the late 19th Century.

In this exceptional collection of short stories, published individually over fifteen years, in parallel with his novels published by the noted French publisher Le Masque, Paul Halter demonstrates time and again the extraordinary range of his imagination and the consistency of his talent. He recreates the fairy stories of his readers' youth; they will go through the enchanted mirror to find the simple joys of their childhood and escape for a few glorious moments the sinister grayness of the adult world.

Readers will find here both of M. Halter's regular detectives: the indomitable Dr. Alan Twist 'a magician who can solve the most complex puzzles' and who has never known defeat; and the art critic Owen Burns, an aesthete who carefully cultivates eccentricity and whose fascinating persona owes a lot to Oscar Wilde. Two detectives with outstanding analytic gifts and who make a point of only investigating 'exceptional cases, mysteries which are beyond our normal understanding; if you will, crime in its most enigmatic—and therefore artistic—form.' Two exemplary characters caught up in stories set, for the most part, in long forgotten times with old-fashioned attitudes. In Twist's case, the England of village life and gloomy haunted mansions, set in the period pre-and post-World War II. And, in Burns's case, the London of the turn of the 19th century, with 'its hackney cabs, gas lamps and fog; its pubs, its easy women, and its dark alleys.' And constant evidence of an extraordinary ingenuity, accompanied by a devastating black humour.

You are invited to follow these two great demolishers of mystery and their confreres who, although amateurs, are fully capable of finding 'a rational explanation for the most unlikely cases and mysterious crimes.' One last piece of advice for the unwary traveler along the paths sketched by our master storyteller: beware of the formidable talent of Paul Halter and his extraordinary gifts of persuasion. He can make you accept the astounding and the unthinkable, and convince you of the wildest impossibilities. To cap it all, in *The Flower Girl*, he will attempt, literally and shamelessly, to make you believe in Father Christmas!

The reader is warned.

—Roland Lacourbe

*The original collection included one story based on an untranslatable pun. That story was dropped and two new ones: *The Abominable Snowman* and *The Golden Ghost* were added for this English version of the collection.

THE ABOMINABLE SNOWMAN

———

Looking back and reflecting on matters, Irving Farrell was inclined to doubt the evidence of his own eyes. The only thing he was sure about was the time: it was around eleven o'clock at night that the stretcher-bearers emerged from the narrow side street. Not only had he heard a nearby church clock strike eleven times, but several witnesses confirmed it. As for the rest of it . . . had he imagined it all? Had he had one of those mysterious premonitions? Or had he simply partaken too liberally of those alcoholic beverages his hosts had so generously supplied? Even so, that would hardly explain the coincidence. Irving Farrell, a small, elderly gentleman, renowned for his powers of deduction, had always insisted that there was an explanation for everything. He was frequently consulted about some apparently inexplicable mystery, which he inevitably solved. What happened in London in the winter of 1929 is a prime example of his abilities, except for that vexing question of the time, which is still not resolved . . .

The extraordinary events took place on the night of a very cold Christmas Eve. Around ten o'clock he left his hosts to go to another appointment. An old friend he had bumped into the night before had invited him to celebrate midnight mass with him. When explaining the shortest route to his house, he had—needless to say—claimed it was very easy to find.

"Just imagine if it had been difficult," Farrell said to himself with some irony, after having wandered for over an hour through the deserted, snow-covered streets of the peaceful area just north of Bloomsbury. Tired and weary, he had the distinct impression of having gone round in circles and was ready to give up, faced with the dreary prospect of endless rows of terrace houses, with their almost identical front doors, iron railings, and snow-capped chimneys.

But behind the brightly lit windows he saw no reflection of his own gloom, only joy. In front of the well-laden tables, and with the benevolent presence of Christmas trees festooned with paper-chains and candles, people were laughing, singing, and even dancing to the tune of an old piano or violin.

It had just struck eleven. After having explored yet another dead end, he was seriously thinking of going home when, under the baleful light of a street lamp, he noticed two ambulance men coming out of a side street carrying a stretcher. He was surprised not to have heard them coming, but attributed that to the noise of the revelers. Their gray shadows stood out against the blinding white of the snow as they worked their way slowly and methodically towards their vehicle. A uniformed constable brought up the rear, as if in a funeral procession. The scene surprised him because he had seen scarcely anyone in the last hour. A lump came to his throat as he realized that the face of the individual on the stretcher was covered. Under one edge of the blanket, he was able to see from the shoes that the body was that of a man. An accident on Christmas Eve? How very tragic.

As the bearers were busy loading their burden into the ambulance, he managed to ask the policeman a question: "An old tramp, dead from the cold?"

"Not a tramp and not old," replied the officer, shaking his head slowly. "Fifty at most, and fairly well-dressed. And we don't yet know the cause of death. A couple of the locals saw him as they were going out. He was slumped in a corner at the end of the street, and just seemed to be in a deep sleep."

"That's all very sad."

"Yes, God rest his soul. Well, goodnight, sir."

So saying, the constable climbed into the vehicle, which drove off leaving Irving Farrell alone in the street, and somewhat perplexed without knowing why. Something had seemed strange to him, but he couldn't quite put his finger on it. He stood looking at the narrow street for a moment, then started down it; after all, it may well be where his friend lived, at the bottom on the right, as he had said.

To his left was a long, high wall without any opening. To his right were four respectable terrace houses, only the first three of which had lights in the windows. The street ended in a blind wall. It must have been somewhere around here that the poor fellow was found, he thought to himself, stopping level with the last house, which was in complete darkness. He struck a match as he bent down to look at the name on the doorbell and gave a deep sigh. It still wasn't the right address. He nearly jumped out of his skin as a voice came out of the darkness behind him:

"Good evening, sir. Are you looking for someone?"

He turned quickly round. The man facing him was of medium height, hatless, and wore a coat with an astrakhan collar. A pencil moustache gave him a certain distinction and, as far as could be made out in the darkness, he had a pleasing countenance.

But where the devil had he come from? Farrell was certain he hadn't passed anyone in the narrow street. Unless he was already at the end of the street in the unlit corner, in which case, what was he doing there alone in the darkness?

"Yes, but it seems I must have the wrong address," replied Farrell, keeping his eyes on the stranger. "But tell me, sir, do you know who was the poor unfortunate that they just took away?"

"I beg your pardon?" exclaimed the stranger, in apparent surprise.

"Yes, that fellow who had passed away and was just carried out of here five minutes ago. He must have been found lying around here somewhere."

"I'd be very surprised at that, because I've been here for a while. I haven't seen anyone. Nobody; not a single soul."

"Well maybe it was further up, at the top of the road?"

"No, I would have seen that, too. You must have been mistaken, sir."

Farrell's first thought was to protest strongly, but the stranger's calm assuredness caused him to reconsider. He began to wonder: had that strange funeral procession been merely a figment of his imagination, born of fatigue due to his long and fruitless wandering in the cold weather? Besides, his instinct—which rarely failed him—had told him something wasn't quite right.

"Yes, well, I must have been mistaken," he conceded. "I've been mistaken all night, for that matter, what with these houses that all look the same. I'm looking for a friend of mine, whom I thought I had found just now, in the next street—like this, the house at the end."

"Yes, I see," acknowledged the stranger. "That would be where the Wilsons lived. But they weren't at home that night."

"Which night?

"Christmas Eve, ten years ago. A dreadful night because of the horrible event, right here where we're standing."

The man turned and, with his gloved hand, indicated the dark area at the end of the street.

"It was right there that the tragedy occurred. The victim was found in front of the wall at the end, savagely murdered."

"So there was a body!" said Irving Farrell with a shudder.

"Yes, no doubt about it."

"And a body taken away by the ambulance men?"

"Of course, just like all bodies. But this was ten years ago, my dear sir."

For a moment, Farrell stood frozen like a statue. His eyes gradually became accustomed to the half-light. The light from the first houses now illuminated the darkest parts of the dead-end, which yielded up nothing remarkable: a banal view of a brown wall rising from a blanket of virgin snow. Yet there lingered an indefinable sense of something unreal, perhaps due to the presence of this strange individual, or maybe because of the ghostly handful of snowflakes swirling in the semi-darkness.

"So was it a hallucination, or did I perhaps see ghosts?"

The stranger stood staring at the scene of the crime, apparently not hearing the question. In contrast to Farrell, shivering despite his thick overcoat, he seemed oblivious to the cold. After a long silence, he said in a lugubrious voice:

"Ralph was tried and hanged for the crime, but I know he didn't commit it. He proclaimed his innocence right up to the moment of death. I come here every year in the hope that someone will lift the veil of mystery."

"The mystery of the murder?"

"Yes. Because all the signs were that it was the work of a ghost. According to the evidence, only Ralph could have committed the crime. That's what sealed his fate. Because it seemed impossible to envisage how any other human being, no matter how ingenious, could have physically committed the crime."

"Even so, it's a possibility you haven't completely ruled out, if I'm not mistaken?"

"So far the mystery remains unsolved, alas!"

"You know, even the best guarded secrets are revealed eventually."

The man in the astrakhan collar seemed surprised and amused.

"You seem very sure of yourself, sir. On what grounds, may I ask?"

"There's always an explanation for everything."

A challenging gleam came into the stranger's eye.

"Well then, if you have the time, I would be happy to describe the problem to you. I can't believe you'll solve it, but if you do you will have done me a great service."

Irving Farrell's wrinkled features cracked in a mischievous smile:

"Actually, I have all the time in the world now; I've given up any hope of finding my friend tonight." He rubbed his hands together and blew on them vigorously. "I'd have preferred to do it in front of a roaring fire, but go ahead, I'm listening."

After a lingering look at the silent house, the stranger started his tale:

"Let's begin at the beginning. I don't know who lives in that house today, but it's not important. There's an air of sadness about it, as if it has been tainted by past events. But there was a time when it was full of contentment and well-being. The Graves family lived there. John Graves was a serious man, a civil servant devoted as much to his government service as to his family. And his wife, Mrs. Esther Graves, was likewise above reproach in every regard. They had three children: two sons, Fred and Hugh, in their twenties, and the last-born, Jessica, a shy but pleasant girl who liked nothing more than to shut herself in her room with her dolls.

"Everything was going well enough until the beginning of 1914. The two brothers had recently met a certain Maude Faulkner, who did not lack for admirers, and both had fallen madly in love with her. With her heart-shaped face, boyish haircut, and luminous dark eyes, she was a ravishing creature indeed. Fred, handsome, fair-haired and a great storyteller, was far more extrovert than his rather reserved brother. Hugh, tall and dark-haired with soulful eyes, had the more romantic nature. He seemed overshadowed by his elder brother—older by only a year—yet it was Hugh that won Maude's heart and they were married just after the start of the war. All three of the Graves men took part in the conflict but only one survived. John was killed during a bombing raid and Hugh, who fought side by side with his brother at Ypres, was mortally wounded during a German offensive. Fred was therefore the only one to return in 1918 when the hostilities ended.

"His presence was a great comfort to his mother, who never got over the death of her husband and younger son. Maude had seemed stricken when she learned of the death of her young spouse, but her youth and the short duration of her marriage spurred her recovery, greatly aided by the attentions of the survivor. So much so that, within less than a year, she and Fred began planning their engagement. In some ways this was a comfort to everyone, including Mrs. Graves, who had become accustomed to the presence of the young woman in the family home.

"Maude had an elder brother, Jerry, who had also fought in the war. On his return from the Belgian front, he had been somewhat at a loss about his future because his parents had both died while he was away. So he accepted Mrs. Graves' offer to stay with them while he recovered his health and found a job. He had brought back a terrible souvenir of the war: a piece of shrapnel buried too deep in his head to be operable. He suffered frequent and violent attacks of migraine, which prevented him from holding down a regular job such as the civil engineer he had once been. Nevertheless, he was an amiable fellow, resembling Hugh in some ways, though older. He seldom went out, and spent most of his time reading whenever his migraines permitted.

"I must also tell you about the Vances, father and son. Captain Charles Vance, long-time friend of the late John Graves, was Hugh's godfather. He also had returned wounded from the war, and would henceforth always walk with a limp. Rather gruff in his manner, he nonetheless had a good head on his shoulders and was a man in whom one could have complete confidence. Since the death of his old friend, he had taken it upon himself to watch over the family and was a frequent caller, always checking that all was well. He was never to be seen without his son Basil, a skillful young surgeon, who showed a keen interest in the equally young Mrs. Graves, still as lovely as ever despite her widowhood. Basil was a gentleman of impeccable manners: a delightful fellow appreciated by all. He was over thirty, just like Jerry, and I believe that Maude would have succumbed to his charms had it not been for the presence of Fred, who was pursuing her in a determined manner. Fred, in those days, was a mere typewriter salesman and was doubtless interested in Maude's personal fortune, inherited from her parents, as a way of furthering his ambitious projects. But let me get to the first strange incident, which occurred a month before the fatal event, in November, 1919.

"One night, Maude woke up suddenly, in the grip of a frightful nightmare. She had seen Hugh, who had appeared to her as a ghost, dressed as a soldier. He was brandishing a rifle with fixed bayonet, and crying vengeance as he walked menacingly towards her. Fred tried to reassure her: it was just a nightmare, as many young widows in her position must have experienced. Which was clearly true, but people would later remember that strange dream.

"That year, the winter was harsh. There were frequent heavy snows. Jessica, who had remained a child at heart despite the fact that she was nearly fifteen years old, showed unabashed delight in playing in the snow. She had built a huge snowman there, at the end of the cul-de-sac, and was very proud of it. She gave strict orders that nobody should go near it; orders which were respected from the start. However, as if to underline the warning, she had seen fit to deck her work with the helmet and jacket of her late brother, which the army had returned along with the dead man's personal effects. Furthermore, she had placed a bayonet in the crook of its arm, and while in broad daylight it merely looked grotesque, after nightfall it became sinister and menacing. The helmet and bayonet undoubtedly provoked strong feelings in the household.

"Mrs. Graves didn't like it. Her initial reaction was to have the snowman destroyed but, faced with floods of tears from Jessica, she relented. Fred, also, became very angry about the matter, but Jessica managed to calm him as well. Normally a quiet person, she became a veritable tigress whenever her little universe was under threat, be it her dolls or any other of her personal things. To cap it all, she even went so far as to name her snowman 'Hugh'. All that I've described took place at the beginning of the fatal week and affected the entire household. For example, the evening after 'Hugh' was built, Maude received a severe shock as she was entering the house: she was sure she had seen the snowman move. Of course, it was just a figment of her imagination . . . at least I assume so.

"Three days before Christmas, Maude, Fred, Jerry and Dr.Basil Vance went into town to attend a party thrown by friends. The event was important because it was where they met Ralph Peterson, a young and rich farmer from the north, who had known the Graves brothers during the war and had actually fought alongside them. His languid drawl, curled moustaches and slightly crossed eyes behind silver-rimmed spectacles made him hard to ignore, added to which he was an uninhibited party-goer. He went straight for Maude, somewhat to the amusement of Fred, who had not yet made his engagement plans known and clearly didn't consider Ralph a dangerous rival. On the contrary, his old comrade-in-arms' clumsy efforts brought him to the brink of tearful laughter. Maude herself joined in the fun, flirting with Peterson and pretending to be fascinated with his new and flamboyant attire.

"'You have the most striking outfit of the evening,' she gushed, after rapidly downing a glass of champagne. 'Where did you find it?'

'In town, actually. This morning, as a matter of fact. Pemper & Boyle in Regent's Street. A little bird told me I was going to meet someone special tonight.'

'Your shoes are extraordinary, too.'

'Extraordinary—and extraordinarily big!' said Fred, slyly.

'Size twelve. Bought them in the same place, don't y'know.'

'And that, um . . . amazing shirt, too, I'll bet.'

'Quite right. Never shop anywhere else. When I see something I like, I just buy it. No point in messing about.'

'Oh?' said Maude. 'And do you like me?'

'Oh, I'll say. Rather a lot, actually.'

'So what are you prepared to pay?'

'All the gold in the world, my sweet.'

"That gives you some idea of the tenor of the evening, with everyone throwing themselves into the spirit of things. But then Ralph made a startling remark. While Fred was dancing with Maude, Ralph, who was at the bar with Basil and Jerry, and decidedly in his cups, took the others into his confidence.

'Yes, I knew the Graves brothers very well, particularly Hugh, who got himself shot, poor fellow. By the way, do you know what some of the chaps were saying about him? It's a bit off talking about it, particularly when one isn't sure about anything. But, on the other hand, one can scarcely keep quiet because—Well, dash it! Some were saying it wasn't a German bullet that got him.'

'What do you mean by that?' asked Basil.

'Speaking personally, old boy, nothing,' replied Peterson, staring dreamily at Fred and Maude on the dance floor. 'I'm just telling you what some of his comrades were saying at the time.'

The stranger stopped for a moment, as if to emphasise what he had just said. Irving Farrell broke the silence:

"Hmmm. It's a thinly veiled accusation. If the bullet was indeed not a

German one, we must be talking about an assassination. In which case, the culprit is obvious: Fred, who used the opportunity to eliminate his rival, the brother who had taken the woman he loved and who could now be his. Yes, Maude's nightmare is more readily understandable now."

"Exactly, I must tell you that even before Peterson's remarks, rumours had been circulating, but nothing definite; people had dismissed it as baseless scandalmongering. But now, with this new first hand account, things were different. Nobody spoke about it in the Graves' house, however. One could have supposed that it was because they were simply unaware, Jerry and Basil having kept the confidence. But that was far from being the case. Jerry had probably told his sister, and Basil his father, because the talk eventually reached Fred's ears, upon which he roared with laughter. Perhaps to prove his detachment, and hence his innocence, he decided to invite Ralph to drop by after dinner on that fateful Christmas Eve. And now we get to the tragic moment . . .

"It had snowed the whole day until nightfall and the whole street was under a thick carpet of snow. The Graves family and their guests, Captain Vance and his son Basil, had just finished eating around 9 o'clock when the first incident occurred. A fuse blew and the corridor, the kitchen, and the hallway were plunged into darkness. There was no spare fuse and the family was prepared to leave it until the next day when Captain Vance, sure that he had several spares in his house in nearby Russell Square, insisted on going to fetch them despite his limp and his friends' protests. 'A little exercise will do me good after that banquet,' he said as he left at around 9.30.

"He didn't pay any attention to 'Hugh', the snowman, still standing there at the end of the cul-de-sac, an absurd motionless sentinel with his useless helmet and bayonet. No more, apparently, did Ralph when he arrived at the Graves' house at 10.15. Jerry answered the doorbell and asked Peterson to wait in the drawing room, because Fred was noticeable by his absence. 'He must be upstairs, probably in his bedroom,' Jerry was heard to say as he went out, leaving the visitor alone.

"At this point I need to describe the layout of the house and where each individual was to be found at the time. When you enter by the front door you see over there, you find yourself in a small hall leading to a long corridor on your left which runs parallel to the street and gives access to all the ground-floor rooms. So, on the side facing the street, you find, respectively, the dining room, the library and the drawing-room where Ralph was invited to wait. That's the furthest window you can see and the closest to the dead-end, and which therefore directly overlooked the spot where the snowman was standing.

"Dr. Vance had stayed in the dining room to smoke a cigar. Mrs. Graves was in the kitchen opposite, across the corridor. Having dismissed the maid at the start of the evening, she was preparing the coffee herself, by the light of the chandelier. She heard Peterson arrive and caught a glimpse of him talking to Jerry. Maude was looking for a book in the library, in order to research a point about South African tribes arising from a discussion with Basil.

"A staircase in the hall led to the first floor which was laid out the same way as the floor below. There seem to have been only two people there: Jessica, who had gone back to her dolls, and Jerry, who had announced that he was going upstairs to look for Fred.

"According to Peterson's own account, having just arrived, he was in the drawing room listening to the soft tinkling of a musical-box when he heard shouts coming from outside. Going to the window, he was astonished to see Fred in the street battling with a strange assailant: none other than the snowman itself! A snowman in a towering rage, as fierce as a soldier in combat, raining deadly blows from the bayonet down on the hapless Fred! Peterson was so stunned that he remained transfixed for several seconds before raising the lower pane, the better to see, for he had great trouble believing the evidence of his own eyes.

"The nightmare was nevertheless real. As he watched, Fred was succumbing in the snow to the murderous blows of the demented snowman. The poor fellow could scarcely utter a call for help. Realising that he had wasted too much time, the robust farmer finally acted. The shortest route would have been out of the window and over the railings but that was risky because of the spikes, and he would have spent more time climbing over them than running out through the door. That was what he told the police, who accepted his explanation.

"By the time Peterson reached poor Fred, he was lying in a pool of blood at the 'feet' of his bizarre assailant, quite dead. As rigid and unmoving as before, the abominable snowman seemed once again utterly inoffensive.

Just at that moment, Jerry appeared at Fred's window on the floor above. He anxiously demanded of the young farmer:

'What the devil's going on?'

'Fred's been attacked by the—by the snowman. He's dead.'

'Dead?'

'Yes, killed by that monstrous thing. I saw it with my own eyes!'

'But that's not possible!'

'Come and look for yourself!' shouted Peterson, in angry frustration.

'I'm coming. Don't move. No, on second thoughts, get the police!' And he gave the frightened Peterson directions to the nearest police station.

"According to Basil Vance, he had been alerted by the shouts, had followed the exchange from behind the dining room window, and had seen Peterson move rapidly away from the body to fetch the police. He came out of the room and had reached the front door when he was joined in the hallway by Jerry, whom he had heard upstairs. Maude and Mrs. Graves appeared, followed shortly after by Jessica. Basil didn't lose his calm. His profession had accustomed him to such situations, having assisted the medical examiner on several occasions.

'Stay where you are,' he ordered his friends. 'Don't touch anything. I'm going to have a look.'

"Taking care not to disturb any of the footprints already in the snow, he reached the body, examined it briefly, and stood up shaking his head sadly . . .

"It was just as well that he took charge, for the question of the footprints would prove decisive, as we shall see later. The police arrived at ten minutes to eleven. Peterson had not dragged his feet. He was congratulated for his vigilance, but he himself appeared angry about how long it had taken to get the police there. To make matters worse, they didn't believe his story. Their investigation would only serve to increase their scepticism.

"The time of the crime and the cause of Fred's death were not in dispute. The poor fellow had been killed at the spot where he was found, from several blows from a sharp blade, evidently the blood-stained bayonet which was found in the crook of the snowman's arm. The snow had stopped falling in the early evening, so that the footprints found near the victim were perfectly clear and identifiable, corresponding at every point with Peterson's testimony. The area in question extended from the Graves' front door to the dead-end: about twenty-five yards long and six wide. The rest of the street, leading to the intersection with the main road, had been so well-trodden that no identifiable footprints could be found.

"In the section of interest, there were only two sets of prints, if we exclude those of Dr. Vance. Those of Fred, coming from the well-trodden section, and going as far as the snowman. And another set which had gone there and back, obviously those of Peterson. Two Scotland Yard specialists examined both sets carefully and confirmed that there was nothing out of the ordinary about them and that they were, without doubt, those of the victim and the principal witness. Furthermore, no other trace of any kind was found in the surrounding snow. The high wall running the length of the street and the shorter wall across the end were both covered with virgin snow. Nobody could have gone that way. There was nothing suspicious either about the window sills or the railing spikes, each capped with a tiny dome of frozen snow. Simply put, only two people could have reached the victim: Basil and the young farmer. And, according to the doctor's testimony, Fred was no longer alive by the time he got to him. Can you see the problem?"

"Perfectly," replied Irving Farrell with the hint of a smile.

"The scene of the crime lies before you. You can readily see that, under the circumstances, nobody could have got through the walls nor performed any kind of acrobatics from the windows. The fact there was snow everywhere rules out any such theory. And don't forget the testimony of Ralph, who insisted to the very end that Fred had been killed by the snowman before his very eyes. He stuck to his story, no matter how incredible it seemed, and at the risk of his own life. But the police refused to believe him, which was perfectly understandable. You would have to believe in ghosts to accept his story; believe that Hugh rose from his grave to take his revenge against the brother who had killed him for his wife; believe that he had haunted the family home for months before finally taking his rival's life in such a spectacular manner."

Farrell nodded his head pensively, and asked:

"And you, sir, do you believe in ghosts?"

The stranger seemed surprisingly discountenanced by the question, which he evaded.

"I'm sure Ralph was innocent, despite the facts. If he had been guilty, he would never have invented such an unbelievable story!"

"Quite so. And what would his motive have been? To get rid of Fred as a rival, because he coveted the lovely Maude?"

"He claimed he didn't even know about their affair. But nobody believed that either. Anyone could have told him about it during the course of that evening. The police believed that was, indeed, the motive. Or, alternatively, Ralph could have been friendly with Hugh and sought revenge. In which case, it could have been the sight of the snowman—and what it represented—which could have fired his imagination and driven him to create such an astonishing testimony; unless he lost his sanity temporarily after having killed his comrade in arms. But the insanity theory was not accepted ... and they hanged an innocent man."

"And therefore the guilty party is still at liberty."

The man in the astrakhan collar nodded and asked:

"So, my dear sir, do you still maintain there is an explanation for everything?"

"Of course, but I need more information, particularly about the police investigation which, in spite of everything, did look at the possibility of another culprit."

"Just so. Particularly since Ralph's remarks about Fred's odious murder of his brother—in addition to rumours already circulating—could have aroused hatred in any of the family members and a desire for vengeance. I would even go so far as to say that the savagery of Fred's murder by the pseudo-snowman—named 'Hugh,' to cap it all—bears out this theory. Before going over the other suspects' statements, consider Ralph's own, just to understand how hard it is to believe in any kind of conspiracy against him, especially given the speed with which events unfolded. He said that, upon being shown into the drawing room, his eye was drawn to a small painting, the portrait of a young girl, which he said resembled Maude. Just below it, on a low table, were a Hindu statue and a musical-box.

'Whom does it represent?' he asked Jerry, as he sat down on one of the armchairs draped with dust-covers.

'Listen,' said Jerry, opening the box, which started to play a nursery rhyme.

'Very pretty,' said Ralph, 'but I meant the statue.'

'As far as I know it's Kali, the goddess of vengeance. A souvenir of India brought back by Captain Vance, I believe. But you'll have to ask him yourself. Well, I'll go and dig out old Fred.'

"So saying, Jerry left the room, leaving Peterson listening to the gentle music. The guest heard the noises in the street some two or three minutes later, not more. Another minute went by before he went out and found the body. In fact, everything he said was confirmed word for word by Jerry. Unfortunately for him, Maude's brother couldn't have seen the murder. According to Jerry, by the time he had reached the first floor and heard the shouts, Peterson was already in the street standing over the body. According to the police, it was entirely possible therefore for Peterson to have stabbed Fred before shouting out himself. In fact, it's the only theory that explains the crime."

"But what was Fred doing outside at that moment?"

"Only he would have been able to say. Nobody else could describe what he was doing during the half-hour before his death. Basil was in a good position but actually saw no more than Jerry. He heard Peterson run along the corridor, then saw him pass in front of the window. Several seconds elapsed before he heard Peterson call for Jerry, and it was only then that he looked through the window and saw him bending over the body lying in front of the snowman. By the time he went out to examine him, Fred's body was still warm and, according to Basil, had just breathed his last sigh—which, alas! did not help Ralph's case. Basil's father, Captain Vance only came back after the police arrived. He had taken more time than expected to locate the fuses. But, having been absent during the drama, he was of no help to the investigation."

"Maude could have been a prime witness, but she became absorbed in her library research and it was only the hubbub in the house that prompted her to look out of the window. She remembered hearing the musical-box playing, Peterson's hurried footsteps in the corridor, then the shouts from outside. Leaving the room, she came face-to-face with her mother-in-law in the corridor. In the kitchen, Mrs. Graves had just finished her coffee. She had been alerted by the general commotion, without noticing anything in particular except the footsteps in the corridor. Jessica's room upstairs did not overlook the street, so she could not have seen anything. She had vaguely heard the rumpus and, not realizing the seriousness of the situation, had simply left her room out of curiosity. By the time she reached the hall and saw the door open, everyone was already standing on the doorstep. I think that's about all there is to say about what happened."

"Hmmm," responded Irving Farrell, thoughtfully. "Under the circumstances, it's difficult to believe anyone other than the principal suspect could be guilty. One could conceive of someone else in the household dressing up as a snowman in order to commit the deed, but then how the devil could they have done it? Physically, it seems impossible on two counts: not only could a hypothetical killer not have got close to the victim, but also he wouldn't have had the time. It's a knotty problem, I agree. Suicide, maybe? It seems scarcely likely, however, given the character of the victim. I assume that possibility was examined?"

"Of course, but it was categorically rejected, given the nature of the wounds . . . But I was forgetting one small detail. The Hindu statue in the drawing room was found on the floor, smashed into little pieces. When questioned about it, Ralph remembered knocking it over when he rushed out of the room to help his friend. He confirmed that it was intact while he was listening to the musical-box. Now, the strange thing is that when all the pieces were collected, they found that one, the size of a nutshell, was missing. Despite an intensive search, it was never found."

"Curious. Couldn't it simply have rolled into the corridor?"

"No, it was nowhere to be found. The whole house was searched with a fine-tooth comb."

"But that's extraordinary!"

"But what isn't, in this whole business? Starting with a snowman turning into a vengeful soldier simply by dressing him in a dead man's helmet and jacket!"

The elderly Farrell held up a hand.

"Stop. Let me think about this for a moment. The disappearance of that fragment of statue seems to me to be crucial."

"Why is that?"

"Because there's no explanation for it. Nine times out of ten, it's the seemingly unimportant clue which unlocks the mystery. Wait a minute, let me go over all the evidence and try to separate fact from appearance. I noticed that everyone was in agreement—which is unusual—except on one point: the length of time it took for the police to arrive after Peterson went to get them. According to him, it took a long time, contrary to what the others said."

A gleam of amusement came into the stranger's eyes.

"He seemed to lose his notion of everything that night, even his head! Why on earth did he cling to such an unbelievable story. He'd have been better off insisting that he thought he'd arrived at the Graves' house at 9.55 and not 10.15!"

"What? Why didn't you tell me that?"

"Well, I did now."

"Are you sure about that?"

"Of course, because . . . "

He stopped when he saw the ironic smile on Farrell's face.

"You're one of the people in the story, aren't you?"

"To be or not to be, that is the eternal question."

"Don't be shy, Mr.—Mr.—Let's see, simply based on age, you must be either Dr. Basil or Maude's brother."

The stranger pulled up his astrakhan collar and smiled.

"What if I am? That doesn't get you any closer to solving the puzzle."

"Tell me what happened to each of them afterwards. That will give me time to think."

"If you wish. I'll start with Mrs. Graves, who is no longer with us. She died of pneumonia four years ago. Jessica married a French architect, went to live there, and seems happy enough. She wrote to me once to tell me her husband's hobby was making doll's houses. Jerry was never able to get a job because of his severe migraines. He lives frugally on the war pension he was eventually given. Dr. Vance married Maude a year after the tragedy. Their happiness was short-lived. Two years later, Maude died giving birth, as did the new-born. Basil never got over it and still lives with his old father."

"I think you know the truth, sir," said Irving Farrell solemnly.

"Oh? What makes you say that?"

"You've given me every bit of information I need to solve the puzzle. You've summarised everything clearly and completely. The Wilsons' absence; the shorted fuses; the broken statue; the painting; the musical box; Peterson's new shirt and shoes . . . nothing has been left out! It's obvious that you know everything. And now I know who you are."

"That's not very difficult. You have a fifty-fifty chance!"

"Oh, no, not any more. You're Maude's brother, Jerry Faulkner."

The man in the astrakhan collar asked, with a sphinx-like smile: "What makes you so sure of yourself?"

"I eliminated Dr. Vance."

"Why?"

"Because he's innocent."

There was a long silence before the next question.

"So, you understand?"

"Yes. But I warned you, didn't I? Even to the missing fragment of statue."

"Do you know where it was?" said the other, defiantly.

"Yes, on the drawing room floor. The Wilsons', not the Graves'."

Jerry Faulkner looked at Farrell in amazement.

"Hell's bells! You really are a wizard."

"No, sir. I may look like one with my wizened features. But listen to me. Just as I said, you told me everything I needed to know, including the crucial fact that the Wilsons were away that night; the Wilsons, who live in an identical house, but on the next street. As you may have noticed, I am uniquely qualified to attest that all the streets and houses around here look the same! It was over there that you put on your little show, and diabolically clever it was, I must admit. A show which took place twenty minutes before the main event, if I may call it that. You arranged for Peterson to go there and not here, probably by giving him the wrong directions, rather like my own friend (who is presumably still waiting for me, by the way).

"But let's start with the motive. It was Fred, your accomplice, who hit upon the idea of playing a practical joke on Peterson, a very naïve individual, to pay the conceited fellow back for flirting so outrageously with his fiancée. Make him believe he'd been witness to an incredible murder, so that he would go to the police with the utterly unbelievable story and make a complete ass of himself. How ashamed he would be when the officers visited the Graves' house to find no victim and no vengeful snowman! Peterson would pass for a demented storyteller and hence anything he said about Fred's past attack on Hugh would be dismissed out of hand. And that was Fred's real motive. When he asked you to help him, you accepted, but with the thought in the back of your mind that you yourself could use the occasion to get rid of him. Because you didn't like him: you found him too arrogant and too sure of himself. In fact you had hated him since you learned of his treachery. You were not going to allow your sister to marry a murderer. Perhaps you thought of what you were going to do as a sacrifice on the altar of the Faulkner family?"

"I didn't want the other fellow as brother-in-law either, no matter how rich he was!"

"Rich, maybe, but innocent. And his death has weighed on your conscience, hasn't it?"

Jerry Faulkner swallowed, and remained silent.

"So, at 9.55," continued Farrell, "Peterson rang the Wilsons' doorbell. They were probably friends of your parents and had left them their key so as to keep an eye on the premises while they were away. You opened the door and bade him enter their house, which was built and laid out exactly as the one over there. But unfortunately not everything could be identical, including the décor and furniture in the hall and corridor, which were therefore kept in near-darkness—and we can now understand why the electricity failure in the Graves' home had to be engineered. You invited him into the drawing room, which presumably resembled the Graves'; maybe you brought the dust-covers yourselves? In any case, you certainly brought the painting with Maude's likeness, the Hindu statue, and the musical-box—items that he would be certain to remember—to distract his attention from the rest of the room. The goddess of vengeance, the delicate music creating a special ambiance: it was cleverly planned.

"Outside, where another snowman had been built and decorated with cardboard helmet, cape, and bayonet, Fred faked an attack—doubtless wrestling with that great lump of snow and pretending to be stabbed before falling to the ground. Peterson rushed to help him, avoiding jumping over the railings as you had rightly predicted, while Fred played the dying man. You appeared at the upstairs window and went through your patter. Everything went off as planned and Peterson ran off to fetch the police.

"For you and Fred, it now became a race against time. You got rid of the snowman with a few well-placed kicks and destroyed the false helmet, cape, and bayonet. You collected the dust-covers, the painting, the musical box and the statue, which had unfortunately been smashed by Ralph. You swept up the pieces, but didn't have time to check if they were all there, so that one crucial fragment was left behind. You rushed back home and started the second part of the charade, which was much more tricky. After everything was back in place in the drawing room and the bits of statue scattered on the floor, Fred rang the doorbell at 10.15., which left you twenty minutes to do what you had to do. Tight, but doable. You hurried to open the door, and didn't have much trouble fooling your mother-in-law in the semi-darkness. For Fred was wearing a false moustache and round silver-rimmed spectacles just like Ralph, whose almost comical personality was easy to imitate. You made as if to lead him to the drawing room, but in fact you dispatched him outside with orders to put a little blood or a trace of red matter on the bayonet. You quickly donned the shoes you had bought the previous day, which were identical to Peterson's: not difficult because he had innocently provided you with the size and place of purchase during the dance night.

"Then you ran noisily outside to meet Fred, who was by the snowman. Naturally, people assumed the footsteps were Peterson's. In cold blood, you stabbed Hugh's killer several times with the bayonet, which you then put back in place—the whole thing took no more than a few seconds—and pretended to carry out a conversation with yourself, while you removed the spectacles and false moustache and donned them yourself. Witnesses assumed you were at the upstairs window, whereas obviously there was no-one there. Ralph's affected accent was easy to imitate. You simply repeated, word for word, the conversation you had had with him twenty minutes earlier. It was very craftily done, because if anyone had suspicions, Ralph's own testimony—since he sincerely believed things had happened that way—would have reassured them. And, of course, he would have been right—except they had happened in another street twenty minutes earlier. Once you saw Dr. Vance's silhouette at the window, indicating that the matter had his attention, you pretended to go to fetch the police—exactly what Peterson had done. But in fact you ducked back into the house and just had time to hide in the stairwell before Basil came into the hall. You got rid of your disguise and went out to join him. Once again, he behaved exactly as you expected, in a professional manner, forbidding you to go near the body. And the job was done.

"When Peterson arrived with the police—who knew where the Graves family lived and had no need for Ralph's directions—he had no idea that a deadly trap had just closed on him. In front of the snowman lay Fred's body, with his own footprints clear in the snow and those of Peterson going there and back. Of course, the prints were made by your own shoes, which were identical to his. There again, Peterson saw nothing unusual, having made the same tracks himself. One can understand now why the time had seemed so long to him and so short to the others. He had left the false scene of the crime at about 10 o'clock and had returned with the police at 10.50, taking nearly an hour in all. The Graves family, on the other hand, thought he had left at 10.20 and had taken only half an hour. I realized from the beginning that there was a problem of time . . . "

Jerry Faulkner heaved a deep sigh.

"Well, sir, I take my hat off to you. Your deductive faculties are remarkable."

Farrell smiled weakly.

"I think all the credit should go to my friend, with his complicated directions. Thanks to him, I realized that all the streets look the same. That was my first clue and the rest gradually fell into place."

When Jerry Faulkner spoke again, it was with a voice full of contrition:

"Please understand, sir, that I had already been told, at the time of the incident, that my days were numbered and that I would not survive my wounds for long. All the specialists I saw repeated the same thing. I was supposed to be beyond help, yet time passed and I was still there. Several times I tried to confide in someone to assuage my guilt, but could never summon the courage even though I would have welcomed help. Through the years, my headaches got worse. Peterson's sentence of death affected me more than I thought it would. I rarely sleep now and, when I do, my dreams are filled with that damned snowman dressed as a soldier, my monstrous act, and the hanging of an innocent man. Now that someone knows the truth, I know that I can leave with my spirit in peace, for I haven't much time left."

In the darkness, Farrell could hardly see Faulkner's face. After a long silence, the bells of the nearby church started to strike midnight. Their cheerful sound reverberated strangely in the cold of the night, at the end of that snow-covered street still steeped in the horror of bygone events.

"Leave me now, if you please," murmured Faulkner, turning away.

Farrell nodded in response, turned on his heel and went slowly up the street. When he next turned round, he could no longer see Jerry Faulkner. Perhaps he had lain down in the darkest corner, at the foot of the grim wall.

It was not entirely dark, and he should have been able to see him . . . No matter. His limbs were numb with cold and he was in a hurry to get back.

The next afternoon, Irving Farrell was reading the newspapers in the comfort of his hotel room. A paragraph caught his attention. The body of an unknown man had been found in a cul-de-sac in Bloomsbury. It was apparently Maude's brother, yet one important detail did not fit the facts. Hastening to Scotland Yard, he found an inspector who was able to confirm that the body was indeed that of Jerry Faulkner.

"Are you sure of the time, Inspector?" he asked.

"Yes, quite sure. When the ambulance men took him away, he'd only been dead a very short time, probably from a brain seizure."

"You're certain that it wasn't past midnight?"

"Absolutely. There's the constable's report and the ambulance driver's, not to mention the mortuary attendant. They're all quite clear. It was 11 o'clock, no doubt about it. I don't understand your question, sir. Didn't you tell me yourself that you saw them there at that time?"

THE DEAD DANCE AT NIGHT

———

"Up until now, we have always been able to find a rational explanation for even the most baffling and mysterious crimes. I fear that will not be possible in the case I have the honour to put before you. We can automatically rule out a macabre joke from a human source. Whenever people speak of ghosts, it's always about white sheets, clanking chains, and sepulchral moans. That's the classic picture, but it's false. They can make an appearance in a different way, rather like us—the living: singing, laughing, dancing, in other words, having fun. Even indulging in orgies! What happened in the family vault of David Simmons, an old friend, surpasses all understanding. As you will see for yourselves, the absence of human intervention is proved beyond any doubt. Here are the facts . . . . "

Such were the words which Percy Lloyd spoke, several years earlier, in the back room of a restaurant in Piccadilly, to describe the extraordinary puzzle that no Murder Club member had ever been able to explain. This strange club, whose goal was solving unexplained crimes, met twice a year under the honorary presidency of Dr. Twist, the renowned criminologist. Scotland Yard was in the habit of calling upon its star member, and it was always with the greatest respect and pleasure that the celebrated London police welcomed his tall, thin form into their corridors, his friendly face topped by a shock of grey hair, the full moustache above child-like lips and, behind pince-nez attached to a black silk ribbon, a pair of blue-gray eyes sparkling with a mischievous brilliance.

But for now, Dr. Alan Twist was not smiling. He was staring perplexedly at the engine of his car. Ignoring the gusts of rain which lashed his face, he shone his flashlight on it from different angles in a vain attempt to identify the part responsible for the breakdown. A purely reflex gesture, since he knew next to nothing about the subject. He finally gave up in exasperation and took stock of the situation, which was anything but happy. At ten o'clock at night, he found himself in a remote corner of Devonshire and probably condemned to stay there, for he hadn't seen a single vehicle in the last hour. What a great idea it had been. Get away from the polluted atmosphere of London and grab a generous gulp of country air; well, it had certainly been generous. He stood for a moment, listening to the trees moaning under the assault of the wind, when he remembered having seen a house shortly before his car had died on him.

He retraced his journey and walked almost a mile before seeing the gate of a large property. It was half-open; there was a bell, but it was out of order. He set off along a path bordered by old oaks that formed a canopy above his head, and eventually reached a vast lawn, in the middle of which stood an imposing edifice.

He was gripped by a strange, indefinable sense of unease. The darkness, the rain, the moaning of the wind in the age-old trees: all of that undoubtedly made an impression, but he was not about to let it affect him, that would be ridiculous!

To his left, a paved pathway led to what he took to be a small chapel. He stayed a moment to contemplate it, then hurried towards the front entrance of the house. There was a sliver of light at one of the windows. With a sigh of relief, he pressed the button for the doorbell, which shone in the beam of his flashlight. A few moments later, steps sounded in the hall, and the door opened to reveal a relatively young, blond man with a pleasant face and fine features, but with sad, empty, disillusioned eyes which Twist had seldom seen in someone of that age—no more than forty. He explained what had brought him to the place.

"Lucky for you that you noticed our property, because the nearest village is a dozen or so miles away. Come in, sir, and take shelter."

"If I could use your telephone to call a taxi . . . "

"A taxi? You will be our guest, sir, if you will do us the pleasure, and we will sort it all out tomorrow. Don't worry about your car, nobody ever passes through here . . . at night. But permit me to introduce myself: I'm David Simmons."

A quarter of an hour later found Dr. Twist warming himself in front of a blazing fire, a glass of grog in hand. David Simmons had introduced him to the two other occupants of the house: Mrs. Arabelle Simmons, his mother, and Maggie, his twin sister—unmarried like himself. Their resemblance was striking: the same features, the same blue eyes, the same expression.

PAUL HALTER

Mrs. Simmons, who appeared to be of advanced years, dozed in her rocking-chair, eyes half-closed, a woollen blanket tucked under her chin. Her face appeared sculpted out of old ivory, enlivened by the reflection of the flames dancing in the hearth.

As he listened to his host talking pleasantly of one thing and another, Alan Twist began to understand the nature of the disquiet he had felt since entering the house. It was another world, without life, asleep in a bygone age. The rooms with their stale, shut-in smell, the walls hung with faded tapestries, and the furniture old enough to drive an antique dealer crazy. The old lady who looked more like a mummy than a living person. Miss Maggie who, frozen by some sort of lethargy, stared at the flames without seeing them. There was something unreal about it all. But Dr. Twist, whose intuition rarely failed him, sensed that the apathy of David Simmons' sister was only at the surface. "David Simmons", Twist repeated to himself, "wasn't he the Simmons who had been mixed up in that extraordinary business which Percy Lloyd described?"

"It's come back to me!" exclaimed Simmons. "I knew your name rang a bell. One of my college friends, Percy Lloyd, told me about you. You're some sort of detective, aren't you?"

"Criminologist," clarified Twist. "Although I have occasionally been asked by Scotland Yard to give my humble advice."

"Percy spoke about you as if you were some sort of magician who could solve the most complex puzzles, and who had never known failure."

Dr. Twist smiled indulgently and continued tamping down his pipe. In the silence that followed, the crackling of the fire and the wind rattling the windows became more noticeable.

"You have probably observed," continued David Simmons in a monotone, "the strange atmosphere of this house, and its sorry state. We no longer have the means to provide decent upkeep. And soon we shall have to put it up for sale. But will we find a buyer? Who would be mad enough? If you only knew, my dear sir, if you only knew . . . More than ten years have gone by since the terrible events, yet to us it's just as if it were yesterday. The damned past sticks to the skin like. . . . "

"David!" cried Maggie, deathly pale. "I beg you! Don't trouble our guest with ancient history!"

"But it might interest Dr. Twist on a professional level," said David in a soothing tone, as if his sister were prone to fits of anger. "There's no-one like him for getting to the bottom of a puzzle, and his advice could be invaluable."

"There's no puzzle," replied his sister tartly. "As you very well know."

Twist said quietly:

"It just so happens that I know what you're alluding to."

Maggie looked stunned. David frowned.

"Yes," continued Twist. "Percy Lloyd told me about it. His account lacked detail and it was therefore not possible for me to draw any conclusions. But if you describe the events yourself, Mr. Simmons, I might be able to give you an opinion."

Under the triumphant gaze of her brother, Maggie shrugged her shoulders and went back to staring at the fire. David turned to his mother:

"I hope it won't bring back too many memories?"

A half-smile on her lips, eyes closed, the old woman shook her head. David, in turn, concentrated on the flames licking the logs and began his story:

"First, it's necessary to go back about one-hundred-and-fifty years. In those days, the Simmons were among the richest families in the county. Among the richest, but not among the most respectable. Our ancestor Arthur Simmons was a vile, depraved, human being who, having lost his moral compass, threw himself into an endless round of debauchery, as did those who called themselves his friends. His only distractions, apart from hunting and fishing—there's a lake not far from the property—consisted of dissolute banquets and balls, preferably masked. His first wife, our grandmother, died very young. The woman he took as his second wife, and who fortunately did not bear him any children, was his female counterpart. A she-devil, incredibly beautiful, apparently, and with a wild sensuality. Their life together was dedicated to every vice and excess imaginable. Their banquets inevitably ended in orgies, the highlight of which was the diabolical Marion's famous 'necklace dance', so called because that was all she was wearing at the end. It was a heavy necklace, mixing common glass pearls with semi-precious stones, polished and roughly mounted on metal, which gave it a primitive and barbaric appearance. Did she have it made for her? Very probably.

"But there is a natural justice and it all finished badly, very badly. One day, Arthur and his wife were found, together with his brother—who was no better than he was—and his wife, writhing in the throes of a cruel agony. At first, alcohol abuse was suspected, but it turned out they had been poisoned. Was it by a vengeful hand guided by jealousy—always supposing that was a sentiment of which they were still capable? A collective suicide, a sort of supreme ecstasy during the paroxysm of their madness? Nobody knows. Lying naked on the floor, twisting in anguish, Marion broke that extravagant and evil necklace in her last convulsion. Before death finally took her away, she was able, between curses, to convey her last wish: she wanted to be buried with her necklace. So all the scattered bits and pieces were gathered up, in order to put it back together and round her neck once more. All four bodies were buried in the family vault, situated beneath the little chapel—which you may have seen when you arrived here? The dreadful scandal struck a terrible blow to a family esteemed and respected before Arthur Simmons became its head. His son and sole heir had been placed in care by his own mother . . . . "

David's eye wandered to an oil painting of a gentle and charming face, tinged with melancholy, that had drawn Twist's attention because it was the only portrait in a room where everything related to the past.

"Is that the mother?" he asked.

"Yes," replied David Simmons tersely. "Don't be surprised not to see other portraits. Arthur's son burned them all, keeping only this one of his mother, of whom he had no memory of his own. As I was saying, with the approval of his father, who cared little about him, the child was given a home by his aunt, who had hastened to the bedside of her dying sister. His aunt and her husband, a fine and honest gentleman, brought him up to be a man of many accomplishments and he was eventually able to assume his paternal heritage and bring to it some courage and dignity. He and his children worked diligently to blot out the shameful stain on the family name. It was not easy, for strange rumours circulated from time to time. A poacher once claimed to have heard singing and shouts of laughter coming from the chapel! A second account of a similar nature convinced the descendants to open the vault to see for themselves, and even arrange for a local law officer to place seals on the entrance, so as to determine whether the noises were the work of a practical joker. After that, there were—as far as I know—no other such manifestations. But resealing the vault after each new burial became a family tradition. Through the years, the fears faded and the stories became legends. Our late father Henry believed, however, that for the sake of the family, he needed to be above reproach and lead an exemplary life. A sense of honour, respect for oneself and others . . . all very worthy sentiments, but repeated and repeated and repeated, day after day after day, you can appreciate . . . .

"We had an education, my dear sir, of such a rigour and severity as to be almost intolerable."

Maggie nodded with a movement of the head that spoke volumes, and her hands tensed almost imperceptibly. David gave a deep sigh:

"My sister almost never left the house, because my father made all her teachers come here. Our mother was subjected to the same iron discipline. Isn't that so, mother?"

The old lady blinked and pushed back gently on her rocking-chair.

"He thought he was acting for the best. I think he lived in dread of seeing the wild sensuality of 'cursed Marion' manifest itself again in one of us. For him, loose morals in a woman was the deadliest sin. His two brothers, younger than he was, and by no means saints themselves, reminded him of something that our grandfather, a warm and cheerful man, said to him: 'Henry, don't you think there's forgiveness after one hundred years? So, enough of that mournful face.' All the same, he did allow me to go to college and take some pretty challenging courses, which enabled me to escape the confinement of this house for a while.

"Then, one day during the summer vacation, misfortune came knocking at our door, a sign of things to come. One of my father's younger brothers died in curious circumstances. It was during a visit by those two skirt-chasers that Leopold, the younger of the two, passed away. The police were never able to clear up the mystery, because it was proved that the glass containing the poisoned drink could equally well have been taken by his brother. It was as if the murderer had struck at random. So Leopold was interred in the family vault. That's when it all started again . . . .

"Several days later, we were woken up in the middle of the night by the sound of wild, ribald laughter. Only Maggie and I heard the sounds. The following night it was my mother who heard them. She opened the window to find . . . " He paused dramatically. " . . . they came from the chapel! My father, who was in the corner tower—grandfather's old room—which gave an excellent view of any comings and goings over the whole property, was sleeping like a log and she was unable to rouse him, so she woke us instead and we trooped outside with our flashlights. Inside the chapel, there was total silence. We went down the small flight of stone steps leading to the door of the vault, still duly sealed. Not finding anything out of place, we retraced our steps. Just as mother was saying she must have been dreaming—we were at the top of the stairs, a few steps ahead of her—a fearful din from within the vault disturbed the calm, chilling us to the bone. A shadow appeared in the doorway of the chapel. It was father, holding a lantern that illuminated a face frozen in terror. Nonetheless, he kept his head. After having scrupulously examined the seals and finding them intact, he sent me to find a pair of scissors and the key to the vault. The ribbon was cut carefully in the middle and, after the key was turned, the door creaked slowly open. What we were about to find would haunt us all of our days."

David Simmons took a deep breath and continued:

"First, I need to explain the state of the vault and the layout, as it had been the week before, just after the interment of Uncle Leopold. Imagine a long corridor with two rows of niches on each side. No coffins on the floor recesses, because there were still places vacant in some of the upper ones. And yet two coffins from the upper niches had crashed to the ground, and the lid of one of them had broken open, causing the bones to scatter . . . as well as the glass pearls from Marion's necklace! Her name was engraved on the marble plaque in one of the empty spaces above. What had happened here? Had two of the heavy chestnut coffins accidentally fallen? Impossible. The bottom of each niche was flat and perfectly horizontal. But how then to explain the incredible disorder in a vault with no access other than the one sealed door?

"The police were called in, and carefully examined the seals. Apart from the clean scissors cut, they were absolutely intact. No sign whatever that anyone had tampered with them. And that wasn't all! The lids of some of the coffins were not in place as they should have been! They were open and, even worse, some were empty and others contained *two* occupants, placed in a position that—excuse me, Dr. Twist—common decency prevents me from describing. I was horrified and disgusted, and on the point of fainting or vomiting. I closed my eyes, but in my mind's eye I could see the infernal

Sabbath: the coffins opening and the skeletons dancing to welcome the arrival of that joker Leopold, and that brazen hussy Marion.

"Yes . . . but who was the sinister perpetrator of this sacrilege? And how had he got into the vault and out again, without breaking the seals? Those were the questions on the minds of the police. They thoroughly questioned the undertaker's employees and the officer who placed the seals on the vault, to confirm what we had been saying all along: that the vault had been in perfect order when we had left. As a result, I think they seriously doubted our testimony. According to them, somebody shut themselves in the vault at the time of our uncle's interment and somehow slipped out between the time the vault was opened and their arrival on the scene. Which was impossible, because my sister and I kept guard during that time. It wasn't long before they gave up and closed down the investigation. As for us, we had to admit that the old rumours were true: *our family vault was haunted!* And how!

"Father, whose heart was already weak, suffered his first attack. A deeply shameful past, the memory of which he had spent his life trying to erase, had just been reborn. It was beyond his power to control. A second and fatal attack felled him the following week. And that's the whole story, doctor. Once again we have turned in upon ourselves, at a loss to understand. This curse which poisons our lives is based on an orgy which ended in tragedy. The things that were said afterwards don't count for much, because most of it defies common sense. But what we saw ourselves we cannot deny, any more than we can accept it. How many times have I said to myself: '*There are more things in heaven and earth, Horatio, than are dreamt of in your philosophy.*' "

Dr. Twist, who had closed his eyes, the better to concentrate, could not resist joining in the end of the quotation.

"Ah! Mr. Simmons, I see we have the same tastes," he said with a smile. "But let's get to the matter of your uncle's poisoning. Could you be specific about the facts? There was an inquest, I assume?"

David shrugged his shoulders in disillusionment:

"Obviously, if you can call it an inquest. The police simply assumed that it was a suicide. I can still hear them: 'The young people of today are very fragile, that makes the third suicide from depression in a month.' Leopold, depressed? We knew him far too well to believe that was the answer. But could there be another? The crime of a madman, committed at random, just for the fun of it?

"Father, Leopold and Peter were standing here in this room when Janet, who had been in our service for years and was totally above suspicion, brought in the refreshments. Father asked for a glass of port, and Leopold and Peter chose whisky.

"At which point, the three men left the room, for who knows what reason, and returned fifteen minutes later. It was during their absence that the murderer slipped into the room to put poison in one of the whisky glasses. Father sipped the port and Leopold drank from one of the whisky glasses, leaving Peter to drink from the other. I have to stress this point: the glasses were standing on a round silver tray placed on a round table, with nothing to distinguish between the two glasses of whisky, unless it was their position in relation to the port. If Peter had served himself first, we could have assumed he had left the other glass for his brother. But that wasn't the case. All we know is that Leopold collapsed after he emptied his glass."

Twist sat in thoughtful silence for a long moment, then raised his head.

"Very well," he said. "Was there anything else, any odd fact that came to light at that time?"

"Odd fact?" exclaimed David in astonishment. "It seems to me there have been quite enough already!"

"I was thinking of something insignificant, some detail which might have appeared curious without seeming important."

"I can't think of anything," said David, turning to his sister. "What about you, Maggie?"

Her brow creased in a frown as she thought:

"There was that theft that father complained about the day before he died. He wanted to go fishing in the lake to calm his shattered nerves. But he came back furious: his longest fishing rod had disappeared. But it's probably not important . . . . "

"That's not my view," said Dr. Twist grimly. "That's the missing link in the chain."

David and Maggie looked at each other and then turned to their guest in astonishment.

"The missing link in the chain?" repeated David, his eyes bulging. "You . . . Do you mean to say that you have solved the mystery?"

Twist nodded his head solemnly.

"If Percy Lloyd hadn't neglected to tell me a certain fact, I could have worked it out much sooner. He said nothing—either because he wasn't aware of it, or because he didn't think it was important—and that fact was there were pearls scattered over the floor of the vault."

A gust of rain lashed the windows, in just the same way as Twist's words appeared to lash the faces of David and his sister. Mrs. Simmons appeared to be asleep, but the motion of her rocking-chair showed otherwise.

"When you boil it down, this case is actually pretty simple," continued Twist, observing his hosts through his pince-nez. "Let's take the facts in chronological order. There's nothing particularly mysterious about what happened here two centuries ago. The poisoning of your ancestors was probably the result of a jealous rivalry, just as you supposed. And the rumours that followed—regarding the laughter coming from the vault—were not all that unusual given the period, one in which there was a particularly high interest in ghost stories and gothic tales. Any kind of noise at full moon, near a cemetery, would fire up their imaginations and set them off. Moving on to the murder of your uncle and examining the facts, it is obvious that the murderer struck at random and it did not matter whether the victim was Peter or Leopold."

"But that's insane!" exclaimed David.

"Absolutely not! It was vital for the second murder: that of your father!"

"He died of a heart attack, you know," said Maggie calmly, looking at Dr. Twist with a stare which was completely unfathomable.

"I didn't say otherwise. But a heart attack can be brought on by direct provocation, or indirect—as was the case here. The desecration of the family vault was a death blow for your father. A perfect murder. This whole plan was carried out by a master's hand from beginning to end; the first crime— by poisoning, moreover, where it is always difficult to trace the murderer, particularly when the selection of the victim is random—the first crime had as its purpose the death of a member of the family, no matter which, *simply so that the family vault be opened.* After that, the desecration of the sacred place, even though it was a criminal offence, would not have posed much risk for the perpetrator, even if he were caught. Who would dream that these schemes had the sole objective of provoking a fatal reaction from your father?

"Everything seems to indicate that the killer was someone close to him, someone who was aware of his state of health and the moral principles which guided his thoughts and actions. Someone who held a terrible grudge against him. For what reason? The crime speaks for itself. The upheaval in the crypt, mimicking the orgies of his ancestors, was an irresistible shock for such a man: misogynous, puritan, authoritarian, having a complete intolerance for anything, no matter how small, which could be construed as an affront to decency. Someone who must have suffered in silence, without a protest. Someone, therefore, who must be living under the same roof, by his side . . . . "

David crushed the cigarette he had just lit in the ashtray:

"*How?* How could any flesh and blood human being have got into the vault? How, doctor? If you could explain that, I'd be more inclined to believe you."

"Mr. Simmons," explained Twist patiently, "I already told you that one family member was murdered just so that the vault would have to be opened. When the opportunity presented itself, the murderer needed to get into the vault in order to set the stage for later: unsealing some coffins and moving the bodies inside them around. This was the point where the plan was vulnerable, because there was a risk people would notice something while your uncle's coffin was being interred there, but the fact is they didn't. After tampering with the coffins, the murderer had something else to do before the vault was again sealed: prepare the mechanism which would cause some of them to topple over at the appropriate moment.

"Suppose for a second that the coffins were at only a tenth of their normal weight, say between ten and twenty pounds each. The problem would be much simpler. A strong, thin line—such as is used for coarse fishing—could be passed through the coffin handle, then folded in two so that the ends could be brought back and passed under the entrance door, after which a simple pull would displace the coffin and the line could be pulled under the door and subsequently disposed of. Two coffins so two lengths of line, of course. Once the vault was resealed, it would be highly unlikely that anyone armed solely with a lantern would notice the lines, particularly since the killer would undoubtedly have taken the precaution of covering them with dirt well packed down. He would also have taken the precaution of stealing a whole fishing rod, and not just the line, since the absence of the line by itself would have aroused suspicion.

"What moment did he choose to pull on the lines? The instant before you heard the coffins crash down, of course. In other words, just when you were climbing back up the steps. And there the noose tightens: only one of you three could have done it, without running too much risk of being caught, in that place lit only by your flashlights pointing to the exit."

David, who had followed Dr. Twist's explanations closely, observed:

"Well, I must say that solution would work, in a technical sense, if the coffins had weighed twenty pounds. Now I suppose you're going to tell us they were made of very light wood, problem solved?"

"Certainly not," replied Twist, with a thin smile. "It goes without saying, such an obvious ruse would not have fooled anyone."

"So, the problem's still there! How could anyone have toppled those heavy coffins?"

Twist answered with a question of his own:

"Have you ever heard of the wheel?"

"The wheel?" exclaimed Maggie, startled.

"Yes, the wheel, that ingenious invention which allows man to move, if not mountains, at least heavy weights. The wheel . . . or castors! No, there was nothing like that attached to the coffins. But, tell me, what was found in the vault that could have been used as a substitute? You would agree, I'm sure, that if ball-bearings had been found on the floor, questions would have been asked, and it would probably have been concluded that they had been placed under the coffins—easily done, using a lever—to make them roll with a small amount of effort. But there weren't any ball-bearings. So I ask you, what was found instead?"

"Pearls . . . " choked David. "The big glass pearls from Marion's necklace . . . . "

"Exactly. Which was a master stroke by the murderer, because not only did they allow the coffins to roll from their niches, they also inevitably reminded everyone of Marion's infamous orgies and particularly her notorious necklace dance. As always, the best way to hide evidence is to leave it in plain view."

David opened his mouth, but no sound came out. He seemed to be looking about for help, then his eyes settled on his mother, who appeared to be sleeping peacefully in her rocking-chair, now quite still. He got up and went over to her.

"Mother?" he said quietly.

Maggie and Twist came over to his side.

"She has left us," murmured David, visibly upset. "Look, she's smiling . . . as if death had been peaceful and joyful."

Maggie looked long and hard at their guest:

"You think that it was she . . . . "

"The people who had reached the end of their tether with your father were you, your brother, and your mother. I was sure of your innocence and his. There remained the business of the laughter you heard on the nights preceding the macabre event. Now, anyone could have been responsible for the laughter, but only your mother claimed that it came from the chapel . . . and that was obviously a lie."

THE CALL OF THE LORELEI

Under a leaden sky, the white boat full of tourists ploughed through the murky waters of the Rhine. Seated at a table next to the ship's rail, Dr. Alan Twist, a tall thin sixty-year old staidly dressed in tweed, watched the old feudal towns glide past, their haughty silhouettes rising from the brows of the hills, inflexible and uncompromising, underlining the undeniable twilight beauty of the romantic tableau. Did these ancient stones hide the phantoms of the Valkyries? Did they guard the Rhinegold? The elderly British detective pondered these questions, while he succumbed to the strange charm of the legendary river.

Suddenly, a murmur could be heard, coming from the tourists at the bow. Twist followed their gaze and saw, looming out of the mist like a ghost ship, a massive rock, sombre and menacing. The name 'Lorelei' was on everyone's lips.

So this was it. This was where the celebrated siren lured unsuspecting ferrymen to their deaths with her song, wrecking their boats against the rock.

"Awe-inspiring, isn't it?" he observed to his neighbour. "I don't know why, but I've always been fascinated by these old legends."

The man did not answer for a while, until some German tourists had finished singing 'The Lorelei' in their booming voices.

"Old legend?" he said. "Is that what you think? I know someone who did well and truly see the siren."

Dr. Twist turned to the man, a bearded fellow in his fifties with a cynical look in his eye. Nothing in his demeanour suggested he was joking.

"His name was Hans Georg," he continued, his eyes fixed on the deadly rock. "Unfortunately for him, he was unable to resist the call of the Lorelei."

Following this exchange, the detective became friendly with his companion, one Jean-Marie Vix, who promised to tell him the curious tale of

Hans Georg on condition that he visit him in Munchhausen, a small village in the north of Alsace. Twist, who was already on his way to see friends in Hagenau, accepted and eventually arrived at the house of his cruise companion.[1]

Munchhausen is perched on the right bank of the Sauer, which flows into the Rhine farther downstream. The region is fairly wild and often flooded by the tumultuous river, which has created a landscape filled with ponds and tributaries, above which giant willows extend their tangled foliage.

To the north of the village stood the residence of Jean-Marie Vix, in the middle of a dismal heath, beyond the beech grove that sheltered the other houses. It was an imposing half-timbered two-storey house, which did not seem adversely affected by its surroundings. A line of tiles, slightly askew, ran above the ground floor windows. The front door opened onto a wide corridor that ran the length of the house to the back door, the doors to the rooms facing each other in perfect symmetry; the white chalked walls contrasting well with the red of the shiny floor tiles, the half-timbering, and the window-frames of polished wood. The agreeable warmth of the old house felt good to Dr. Twist, as did the amicable welcome of his host as he took his coat and hung it on the coat-rack that stood next to the entrance. On the other side of the door, to the left, Twist noticed some beautiful, long peacock feathers planted in a terra cotta vase standing on a low table, without attaching much importance to them.

His host apologised for his wife's absence. She had been delayed that evening at a town meeting, but hoped that the sauerkraut she had specially prepared would please her visitor. Dr. Twist appreciated it greatly, as well as the *mirabelle* that was served after the meal. That was when Jean-Marie Vix finally began to tell the strange story of Hans Georg.

"It happened back in the mid-twenties. Hans Georg, a young German sales representative, blond and athletic, was enjoying a full life. He was full of confidence in himself and in humanity in general, as if evil had never existed on this earth. During a stay in Munchhausen, he wasted no time in courting my sister Clementine, even though we had only just been freed from the German yolk. Ten years had already gone by since Armistice, but Alsace was still licking its wounds, more deeply than in any other region,

[1] Paul Halter was born in Hagenau

50

because it had paid a heavier price during the conflict. Some of its sons, forcibly conscripted by the Prussians, had been made to confront their own brothers on the field of battle. Our family was not exactly overjoyed, therefore, when Clementine announced her engagement to Hans Georg.

"Pantaleon Vix, my father, was only able to contain his anger thanks to wisdom acquired over the years . . . and a few glasses of *mirabelle*. My mother merely asked her daughter to think carefully about what she was doing. As for me, I was only thirteen at the time and I found Hans Georg to be quite pleasant, with his open manner and ear-splitting gales of laughter. Best of all, he never forgot to bring me a present whenever he came to visit. In contrast, my brother Hubert, only slightly older than Clementine, could scarcely conceal his bitterness. Eventually he calmed down enough to tolerate the German's presence, but he never failed to jeer at our neighbours across the Rhine, as he did on the day when Hans Georg, full of initiative as ever, took us all for a cruise on the river.

"As we approached the Lorelei rock, Hans Georg recalled the old romantic legend. To which Hubert tersely replied that the story had been created from whole cloth to explain the repeated shipwrecks at that particularly dangerous spot. Hans's shoulders shook with laughter as he agreed, after all, that it was highly likely. But shortly afterwards, when the rock came in sight, he stiffened and looked puzzled. It was only on the way back that he confided to us that he had seen a young blond woman sitting on the top of the rock. We took that as a simple coincidence. However, during the following weeks, he thought he saw the young woman several times. In town, in a crowd, at a turn in the road, he saw her making signs at him. Each time, despite his intense curiosity, he had turned away. He felt attracted to the young blonde, but his instincts warned him to be careful.

"For Clementine, the sightings were evidence of a rival, who hoped to lure her fiancé away by some mysterious trickery. Hans Georg was unable to avoid numerous scenes of jealousy. Eventually, however, she agreed with her mother who, ever superstitious, felt the apparitions were a bad omen. In contrast, my father and my brother appeared openly sceptical about the matter. Then winter arrived.

"In mid-December, we celebrated the official engagement of Clementine and Hans. It was bitterly cold. Munchhausen and the surrounding areas were covered in a thick blanket of snow. But here in this house, the ambience was warm and welcoming. There were about twenty of us: our family, some friends, and Joseph, my bachelor uncle, who had limped since being hit by a shell in the trenches. He was an entertaining fellow, who had no equal when it came to livening up an evening with his accordion. For Hans, the vision of the young woman on the rock seemed to be nothing more than a distant memory, as he had not spoken of her for some time. Then Joseph struck up the tune of the Lorelei and a deep chill came over the diners. My parents and the engaged couple went pale. There was a stark contrast between their rigid posture and the lilting sound of the accordion. Uncle Joseph, uncomprehending, nevertheless switched hastily to another song. It was a minor incident which most of the guests scarcely noticed, but from that moment on, Hans gave every sign of being nervous. He tried to remain jovial, but from time to time he could be seen shooting furtive glances at the windows.

"By midnight, everyone had left except Hans. It was still snowing then, but no flakes were falling an hour later when he took his leave. He had kept my father company in the kitchen for one last drink while my mother, my brother, my sister and I myself went off to bed. So, on the stroke of one, he finally left the premises. He left twice, in fact, because he had left his umbrella behind the first time. According to my father, he was the worse for wear but not drunk. He normally spoke very loudly, and so it was that we all heard him proclaim in a thunderous voice: 'Ach! Donnerwetter! Ich habe mein parapli vergessen!', after which the front door slammed a second time. He had put up the umbrella even though it was no longer snowing. My mother was able to observe the strange goings-on from her bedroom window above the front door. The heavy snow clouds had passed, and the veiled moon bathed the landscape in a baleful light. Hans had only gone a few meters in the direction of the village. He turned and seemed to prick up his ears. Then he retraced his steps, hesitatingly. Several times, he seemed to want to set off south in the direction of the village, but each time he appeared to be attracted by a mysterious something emanating from the north. Had he heard the famous siren's song? My mother claimed she did not hear anything out of the ordinary at the time; no song or shout, but as she was half asleep, she couldn't be absolutely sure. She had been aroused from her slumbers by the slamming of the door and the loud shouting in German. So it was that she saw Hans start to walk round the building in an anti-clockwise direction, but was unable to wait for him to reappear, having been overcome by sleep. Hans Georg was found the next morning, drowned in a small frozen pond a hundred yards or so to the north of the house, not far from the Rhine. The wicked siren had finally lured him into her deadly trap!

"The police officer dispatched to the scene that same afternoon conducted a very thorough investigation. As it had not snowed in the interim, he was easily able to reconstruct the route taken by the victim. Hans Georg had indeed walked anti-clockwise around the house, at least as far as the back door. The footprints were not always clear, for the victim had lurched forward and then gone back on his own steps several times, and the snow was not thick due to the overhanging roof. But they became more distinct when Hans had turned determinedly towards the north, even though it was easy to see that the steps were still halting and uneven due to the effects of the joyful evening. Hans had headed straight towards the pond, its frozen surface hidden beneath the blanket of virgin snow. He had known it was there, however, and knew the danger of taking that route, but that had not stopped him from reaching the centre, where the ice had suddenly given way under his feet. During the night, it had frozen again over the body of the unfortunate wanderer, whose outline was vaguely discernable in the dark waters. His umbrella remained on the surface, close to where the jagged edges of the fatal opening had been. The freezing waters must have ensured a rapid death.

"But what inspired Hans Georg to seek such a dangerous place? What had he seen or heard just as he left the house? That was the question the officer asked himself, particularly after having heard about the enigmatic blonde woman who, incidentally, had only ever been seen by the victim. But did she really exist? He firmly rejected the theory of the deadly siren, so dear to my mother and sister. And yet Hans's death remained shrouded in mystery. The idea of a suicide was hard to believe, given the sunny nature of the victim. Hans Georg had no apparent reason to take his life, particularly on the eve of his engagement. An accident? Hardly, given his bizarre behaviour that night. The investigator did not formally advance the theory of criminal involvement, but it must have crossed his mind at some point. Meanwhile, it was firmly established that nobody could have gone near the victim once he had moved away from the house, either to push him in the back or make him fall through the ice in some other way. Similarly, no-one could have walked in his footsteps, backwards or otherwise, the risk being simply too great. Furthermore, the expanse between the house and the pond was completely open. The trees that lined the river bank were too far from the point in the pond where the ice had broken for there to have been any involvement with a tightrope walker, or some other form of flummery. It was finally decided that there had been a momentary delirium brought on by an excess of alcohol, but I can assure you, Doctor Twist, that for me and my family, there was another explanation for Hans Georg's tragic end."

"In short, Mr. Vix," suggested Twist playfully, "you believe it was the siren?"

His companion appeared embarrassed. He stroked his russet beard and sighed:

"Yes, simply because no other conclusion seems possible."

So saying, he took the bottle of *mirabelle*, filled two glasses, and added:

"But something tells me, my dear doctor, that you are not entirely convinced."

"Let's just say that my experience of criminal matters leads me to exercise some caution. But before I share my thoughts with you, I would like to ask a few questions. Can you remember any detail, no matter how trivial, which happened around that time?"

"No, not really," replied Vix, frowning in concentration. "Unless, maybe, the peacock feather, which seemed to intrigue the police officer, but can't possibly be relevant."

"A peacock feather?" exclaimed his guest in astonishment. "Like those I saw in the corridor, near the front door?"

"Yes. The day after the tragedy one was discovered on the floor at the other end of the corridor. My mother had the unfortunate idea to tell the police officer about it, because neither she nor anyone else could explain how it got there."

"How strange. Anything else, apart from that?"

"No, not that I can think of."

"Did Hans Georg speak German with you?"

"Yes, of course," said Jean-Marie Vix with a smile. "He knew a little French, but he assumed as a matter of principle that we could all speak his native tongue perfectly."

"What about dialect?"

"No, nothing. Nothing but German . . . "

"That's what I thought," said Twist, nodding his head. "But there's something strange in your account. Are you quite sure of the words he spoke when he came back to get his umbrella: '*Ach! Donnerwetter! Ich habe mein parapli vergessen!*'?"

"Yes, absolutely, because everyone heard him." His face brightened as something dawned on him: "Ah! I understand, it's the '*parapli*' which puzzles you! Believe me, it wouldn't be the case if you spoke the dialect. Here in Alsace, we use the French word for umbrella; that's probably what threw you off."

"Actually, I think it's the opposite. In other words, because you're used to the dialect, you didn't spot the inconsistency. Think of it: Hans Georg should have used the German word for umbrella: '*Regenschirm*', to go with the rest of his sentence. And yet he did no such thing."

His host seemed surprised:

"Well, yes, I suppose you're right. But there could be a thousand reasons for that." He scratched the back of his head. "After all, he'd had a bit too much to drink that night. But is it really important?"

"I believe so. It could be that someone else spoke those words."

"But that's absurd! Who the devil could that have been, then?"

" . . . And add to that the small matter of the peacock feather," continued Twist, as if he hadn't heard the last remark. "No, it doesn't hang together. Unfortunately, I have too much experience in criminal matters to believe it was the Lorelei."

His host frowned:

"What? Are you suggesting Hans Georg's death was murder?"

"Unfortunately, it's a possibility that can't be ruled out!"

"But then, the murderer must be one of us!"

Dr. Twist emptied his glass with a single gulp, and asked:

"So, what happened to your family after that?"

"There aren't many of us left, alas! Time took its toll, and the Second World War did the rest . . . my brother was shot as a spy by the Germans just before the Liberation. My parents died shortly afterwards, as did Uncle Joseph. Clementine, who had gone to live in Perigord during the hostilities, settled there. Just before she left, she married an old childhood friend from the village. Unfortunately, we see very little of them. Actually, it's very difficult for me to believe that any of them could have committed such a crime."

"Are you quite sure, sir? It would seem clear from your account, nevertheless, that very few of your family approved of your sister's choice. What's more, I just so happens that I know something about the period in question. The defeat in 1870 and the First World War left a great many Alsatians with a lingering hostility towards the invaders. Hans Georg's nationality was seen as an intrusion and a humiliating stain on your family's reputation. It was only his irreproachable manners that soothed their feelings. But it didn't take much to revive the historic hatred. At the end of the day, you are all suspects! Except your sister, because she loved him."

Jean-Marie Vix drained his glass and declared:

"Hans Georg could not have been murdered, Dr. Twist. The investigation proved that officially."

"Couldn't an evil spirit have cunningly lured him towards the pond?"

"By imitating the siren's voice?" replied Vix, with a bitter smile. "I admit I considered that possibility at the time. But there were two reasons against. Nobody in the house heard any such sound, and—let's not forget—there were no other prints in the snow except those of Hans. So I don't see how someone could have enticed him, by the magic of their voice, to walk of his own free will towards the pond, like a sort of zombie under the spell of a song."

There was a malicious gleam in the detective's eye:

"You're forgetting the way he dithered after he went out. Your mother saw him retrace his steps several times before he finally walked round the house."

"Quite so, and there can't be any explanation for that! Which proves we are dealing with a supernatural being."

Twist gravely shook his head:

"On the contrary, there can be a perfectly rational explanation; an explanation which solves the whole mystery, including the *parapli* and the peacock feather."

The silence fell anew, as Vix hung on the detective's every word.

"Obviously, what I have to say is only supposition, but it does have the merit of resolving all the inconsistencies in your story. I'm starting from the premise that Hans Georg was making fun of you with his story of the

Lorelei. During your cruise on the Rhine, he was probably hurt and offended by your brother's remark, which seemed to be directed at the whole German nation. He therefore defended the legend and, in order to convince you, as much for fun as out of spite, pretended to see her sitting on top of the rock. The obvious discomfort of your mother and sister encouraged him to continue with his little game. Your father eventually tumbled to the trick, helped perhaps by Hans Georg himself, who may have admitted it that night, or even boasted about it while they were partaking of their last drink. Your father, his emotions no doubt also inflamed by drink, would have wanted to get even. And at the same time, he must have felt that his daughter's and his family's honour were now in his hands. So Hans Georg was pretending to see the Lorelei? Well then, it was fitting that he should join her!

"After the young man had left, around one o'clock in the morning, he put on a coat similar to the German's, took out an umbrella also similar to his, then shouted that famous sentence in German to draw attention to himself and create the impression that Hans had returned. But he made the mistake I told you about. After that, he left by the front door and played out the pantomime that your mother watched from her bedroom window. With the umbrella up, she was unable to recognise him. He walked round the house, but only as far as the rear door. His hesitant steps and his three-steps-forward-two-steps-back rigmarole served a dual purpose, for they scuffled the footprints so they could not be confused with Hans's, which were quite clear and started from the rear of the house . . . "

"I don't understand. Why that manoeuvre?"

"To make everyone believe that Hans had heard the siren and had not gone straight out by the rear door, which would have seemed strange."

"But what did he do to make sure that Hans Georg went towards the pond?" asked Jean-Marie Vix, his eyes wide open in amazement.

"That's where the peacock feather comes in. As I was walking along your corridor just now, I was struck by how evenly symmetrical it is, with the same number of doors facing each other across the red tiled floor and identical doors at each end. Someone unfamiliar with the premises, or simply disoriented, leaving the house by the rear door and seeing a large expanse of snow with a line of trees at the end, could well believe that they were headed towards the village, because the landscape would seem the same, especially at night and with a mind befuddled by drink. The 'last glass' offered by your father now takes on a completely new significance. It allowed him to take advantage of the individual that he wanted out of his family. To do that, he used an extremely simple but highly ingenious stratagem, and one that only took a few minutes to execute. Making some excuse, he stepped into the corridor and simply moved the coat rack and the low table with its striking peacock feathers from inside the front door to a similar position against the opposite wall at the rear. One feather fell to the floor without him noticing when, later on, he moved everything back. You know the rest: the hapless Hans Georg walked confidently towards his death . . . and joined the other victims of the Lorelei in a watery grave."

THE GOLDEN GHOST

It had snowed almost the whole day. Night was beginning to fall in London but, on that Christmas Eve in 1899, the illuminated shop windows resisted the encroaching darkness like so many candles in an enchanted forest. The shopkeepers had outdone themselves in the ingenuity of their displays. The enthusiasm of the crowds seemed almost to have dispersed the cold. The prospect of the forthcoming festivities and the groaning boards warmed the cockles of every heart.

But the further one went from the city centre, the fewer the lights there were to be seen and the forest of habitations became more somber and more menacing. There were almost no illuminated windows visible, only the occasional gas lamp on the street corner like a pale match desperately fighting the onslaught of the shadows. The happy faces and confident steps of the passers-by seemed to have been engulfed by the cold misery of the squalid streets. The faces were gaunt and disillusioned and the steps were furtive and anxious, for it was not wise to dally in those narrow winding streets, even on Christmas Eve.

Old Charles Godley lived there, in a small shop at the end of a dingy dead-end. In fact, he wasn't all that old: he was approaching sixty, but enjoyed robust health. His height and broad shoulders had made many a ruffian think twice about trying to rob him on a street corner; and the cold, steely look in his little piggy eyes had even caused some to turn tail and run. It was that icy, almost inhuman, regard that robbed his face of any warmth or charm.

As it happened, Charles Godley was nowhere near as poor as his home would have led one to suppose. Far from it: he was exceedingly rich. But in that part of town nobody knew it. He appeared to be just another stingy hovel owner obsessed with his accounts, for anyone venturing to the end of the street would have seen him poring over his books; books which covered every inch of his vast office.

There was paper everywhere. Accounting ledgers, files, and miscellaneous documents were stacked on shelves which groaned under the weight, in improvised stacks, or in cartons which filled all four corners of the room. It was, to the untutored eye, an inextricable mess of papers, but not to Godley, who knew exactly where to find the smallest invoice or the most obscure address of the debtors whom he pursued relentlessly.

Meticulous and pitiless in business, Charles Godley had built his fortune by sheer hard work and indomitable will, dedicating his whole life to it, to the exclusion of all creature comforts. He had never moved from the cold and damp office where he began, and even did without wood and coal for heating. Christmas was perhaps the only time of year when he indulged himself—at least in his own eyes. He usually bought a Christmas tree and decorated it with coloured bits of packing paper—for he considered Christmas decorations a wasteful extravagance—made a fire from a few logs, opened a bottle of sherry, and sat by the chimney to reminisce.

Usually, his friend Sickert came to join him. Under normal circumstances, it would be an exaggeration to say 'friend,' but in this case, given Godley's vague and abstract notions of friendship, it was quite appropriate. Suffice it to say that he appreciated his principal associate's professional qualities, his sound judgment, and his logical reasoning. Besides, he would have been hard put to find another companion for the occasion. Business and friendship make odd bedfellows, he thought to himself in a rare moment of nostalgia.

Slumped in his armchair, the fire warming the glass of sherry he was clutching, Charles Godley felt suddenly overwhelmed by memories. A distant groundswell and faint, for it was necessary to delve far in the past to find any recollection of sensitivity on the part of the man with a heart of stone. He saw himself once again as a child, looking up at the indistinct features of his mother, who had died relatively young. Then the slightly clearer features of a young woman, the only one to trouble his heart enough to make him hesitate, before once more following his chosen path.

It was a strange and disturbing memory, cold yet at the same time feverish, which he had never been able to chase from the hidden corners of his soul. Whenever the uncomfortable thought came to mind, there came also a sense of solitude. Cold hands seized his heart and Charles Godley began to have doubts: doubts about himself, his life, the path he had chosen, and everything else. At this particular moment he could feel some warmth from the fire, yet no matter how many logs he piled on, it could never burn strongly enough for him to feel the comfort of a true family hearth.

As he sat there with his confused thoughts, steps sounded outside in the street. He sat up and strained to hear: the steps were hurried and clearly coming in his direction. Who the devil could it be? He was the only inhabitant of that dead-end street. Could it be his friend Sickert? Then why was he running?

The steps stopped suddenly and there was a frantic knock on the door. A breathless voice implored:

"Open, please open for heaven's sake, or I'm lost!"

Godley frowned, stood up, and walked cautiously to the door as the cries became more and more insistent

"Who's there?" he growled, his hand hovering hesitantly above the door-knob.

"Someone who's going to die if you don't open immediately! I beg of you, don't leave me outside with *him*!"

Despite his suspicious nature, the merchant finally obeyed. On the doorstep he found himself face-to-face with a fair-haired young woman, bedraggled and haggard. She couldn't have been more than sixteen years old and was dressed like a beggar. Under her arm she carried a canvas bag as full of patches as the rags which served as her coat. She was thin and hollow-cheeked and her big blue eyes held the look of a frightened deer.

"Thank God!" she moaned, placing a trembling ice-cold hand on his wrist.

"What's this about?" he asked in a gruff voice.

"*He's* hounding me—"

"Who's *he*? I can't see anyone."

The unknown visitor looked quickly over her shoulder at the silent snow-covered street, and stammered:

"I know. *He's* not always visible . . . but please, sir, let me come in."

The young girl's pleading voice and the look of desperation in her eyes overcame Godley's initial reluctance, but more was to come. No sooner was she inside the house than she demanded he double-lock the door and shoot the bolt, which he did with a calm assurance; but his visitor remained in a state of fear.

"Shut everything, lock everything!" she repeated, while scrutinising the room for any possible opening. "The shutters! Are you sure you've closed them properly?"

"Of course. Always at nightfall," replied the merchant, with barely suppressed irritation. "And now, please calm yourself."

"What's that over there, behind the windows? Is it a door? Does it lead to a courtyard or to the rest of the rooms?"

Godley went over to where she was looking and pulled back two pieces of cloth to reveal yet another bookcase.

"Nothing but ledgers, as you can see."

"So this room doesn't connect with any others?"

"No. My living quarters are on the floor above. I have to climb the outside stairs to get there. Does that reassure you?"

"More or less," she replied hesitantly.

"Well, it's about time. Now, do you mind telling what you're so frightened of?"

"Yes. Someone . . . someone who doesn't wish me well."

"Right. Now come with me," said Godley, marching determinedly to the front door, which he proceeded to unlock and throw wide open.

"But—but are you mad?" asked the young visitor, surveying every nook and cranny in the street as if mortal danger was lurking in the shadows.

"No. Look, there's not even a cat. Now come with me."

"No! No! He'll ambush you."

Godley grasped the girl's hand and, over her protestations, steered her outside, saying:

"Look carefully. Those are your footprints in the snow. They start at the top of the street and you can see there aren't any others. So obviously nobody could have followed you here. Do you want to walk all the way to the end?"

"No, no—I'm cold," said his visitor, looking down, her teeth chattering.

Following her gaze, the merchant noticed she was bare-foot. Surprised, he exclaimed:

"But . . . don't you wear any shoes?"

"Not always."

'What? Not even when it snows?"

"Yes, but I lost them when I was running."

"But you don't lose shoes when you run."

"Um . . . The ones I had were a bit big for me. I borrowed them from a friend this morning."

"And why were you running?"

"To get away from *him*."

"But from *whom*, for goodness' sake? As you can see, there's no-one there.'

The girl stood in silence for a moment. The only light was coming from the shop. It made the snow sparkle and heightened the glow of her blonde hair. Framed by the golden curls, her lovely face, its beauty seemingly heightened by anxiety, contrasted strangely with the leprous walls of the warehouses which lined both sides of the narrow street. Barefoot, and apparently insensitive to the cold, she turned to stare fixedly at the source of the light and replied:

"I told you, sometimes he's invisible.'

"*Invisible?* What are you saying? Is he a man or a demon?"

"I don't know . . . I call him the golden ghost, because when he follows me I can see a golden silhouette. How to describe it? It's as if he's invisible, but he sort of shines in the light. I don't know if I'm making any sense—"

"Yes, perfectly," sighed Godley, placing his hand on his visitor's shoulder. "Come along, I'll find you a pair of slippers and give you a glass of sherry and we'll talk more about it in front of a nice warm fire. You'll see, after that you'll feel better."

A little later, after the young girl had warmed herself and was comfortably installed in an armchair, she was able to talk more calmly about her fears. But her explanation was no clearer for all that.

"He haunts my dreams, but I also see him when I'm awake. It's been going on for a long time, as long as I can remember."

"The devil it has!" exclaimed Godley, seated on his desk chair which he had brought closer to the fire. "It may be more serious than I thought."

While serving his visitor another glass, the merchant started to think, with a sort of ironic detachment, about his own reaction. It was not his habit to be welcoming with strangers—nor, for that matter, with anyone else. So why was he feeling such a strange compassion towards this young unknown person? Was it because of her pretty face, or maybe her distressed situation? Was it because it was Christmas, or was it the strange nostalgia which had seized him earlier that evening? Was it simple curiosity on his part, or was there some other reason?

"In fact," she continued, "he appears mostly at night, when I'm walking alone. He stalks me; he pursues me relentlessly, and when I turn round all I can see is his shining silhouette, as if he was made of a thousand reflections or golden sequins."

"Tell me, does this mostly happen when it's very cold?"

"Possibly."

"In winter, when it's snowing?"

'Now you mention it . . . " she answered hesitantly.

"So maybe it's Father Christmas?" said Godley, mischievously.

The young girl shook her head vigorously:

"No, it's someone evil. It's someone who wishes me ill, I'm sure of it." With a look of disappointment, she added: "So, don't you believe me? Do you think I'm mad?"

"Mad, no," replied Godley, smiling. "But there's good reason to think you may be quite disturbed. The absence of any prints in the snow proves you're not dealing with a normal being, wouldn't you agree?"

"Oh, there's no doubt about that."

"So shall we call it a spirit?"

"A spirit . . . like a ghost?"

"Yes, a ghost," agreed Godley, his face copper-coloured by the flames. "One of those ghosts who seek revenge, for it seems to be a vindictive creature. Unless it just wants to talk to you."

"Then it must be in order to blame me for something," said his guest anxiously, turning her big blue eyes on her host. "My goodness! I must have committed a sin."

"You're the only one who can say, my dear."

"Unless it's the devil himself who wants to make me do something evil."

"Possibly. But in any case, you're going to have to search your past life."

"My life?" she repeated sadly. "I'm afraid there isn't much to tell."

Looking at her, Godley again felt pangs of pity.

"In fact, now that I think about it, you haven't even told me your name."

"Jenny . . . Jenny Brown."

"Jenny Brown?" he repeated, smiling. "That's a common enough name, but a pretty one all the same. Jenny . . . yes, I like that. I can call you Jenny, can't I?"

"Yes, that's what everyone calls me."

"And now, Jenny, tell me everything about yourself and I'm sure that between us we'll solve the mystery of the golden ghost."

Charles Godley, to his bewilderment, found the young girl's story very moving. On that Christmas Eve he had the distinct impression he was changing: that his cold heart was melting due to the contact with this stranger . . . and possibly the warm hearth and the sherry, of which he was now partaking copiously.

Jenny seemed to have been dogged by ill fortune since birth. She hadn't even known her father, who had abandoned her mother when he had learned of her imminent arrival. The unfortunate Mrs. Brown, who had had to work her fingers to the bone to bring Jenny up, had died of pneumonia when she was but ten years old. Subsequently she was placed in the care of a tyrannical guardian who was so severe she preferred to flee and earn her living in the streets. Nights under the open sky, squalid lodgings, and sordid refuges had been the only homes she had known since.

"In fact," she concluded sadly, "I've never had a home and never known a happy Christmas. When she was alive, my mother was so poor that I never experienced warmth or a sense of security."

"I've never had a home either," said Charles Godley, nodding his head in sympathy. "But what do you live on, these days? Are you begging?"

"Oh, no!" replied the young girl. "Mother taught me dignity. It's true that occasionally I've had to accept alms, but I'm actually a merchant."

A gleam of suspicion flickered in Godley's eyes.

"A merchant?" he echoed in astonishment. "What do you sell?"

"I'll show you," said Jenny, getting up and crossing the room, weaving her way between the stacks of paper and the boxes, and bringing back the tattered bag which she had placed in a corner. She opened it for the merchant's inspection; inside was a multitudinous jumble of little yellow boxes which he identified immediately:

"Matches," he mumbled in surprise, as if he had just made a strange discovery. "You sell boxes of matches."

"Yes."

"And does it pay well?"

"Judge for yourself," she replied, looking down at her miserable garments. "But I'm not complaining, for I like my matches. Since I've been selling them, I've come to appreciate them. They are my companions in misery. With them, I'm never completely alone and I'm always warm, even when it's really cold, outside at night."

A touch of bitterness could be seen fleetingly at the corner of her perfectly sculpted lips, but soon a strange contentment suffused her features.

"So I huddle in a corner, I strike them one by one, and I watch them as if I'm in a dream. If I watch long enough, they change into candles: a host of candles forming a staircase up to the sky. Then my heart is warm and I feel much better. I feel I'm in my own sweet little room in a welcoming home, surrounded by a loving family . . . I see my grandmother, my mother, and even my father—although his face is blurred. But I still believe he's happy to be with us. Everyone is happy . . . There's a real fire burning in the hearth. I almost burn my fingers when I reach out to warm them. But how blissful it is after wandering almost frozen in deserted streets. Sometimes the candles form a vague silhouette in the sky, like a luminous ghost . . . "

"A luminous ghost!" exclaimed Godley. "There we are! And I imagine the mysterious creature has been following you since you've had these visions."

"Yes, I believe so. Now I think about it, you were right about what you said earlier: I believe he's trying to tell me something."

There was a sudden knock at the door. It was not loud, but to Godley's ear it had a strange resonance and it made him shiver. For a few seconds, he imagined a visitor with a golden silhouette, but he quickly recovered himself and declared:

'That must be Sickert. I'd completely forgotten about him."

He went to the door, greeted his friend, and made the introductions.

Sickert was solidly built, like Godley, but far better dressed than he. His velvet frock-coat was impeccable and a perfect match for his other clothes. The gold watch-chain across his waistcoat was in itself a provocation in the rough neighbourhood. Raising his top hat, he revealed a shaven cranium above a round and pleasant face.

"Jenny," said Godley, "this is the man of the moment. Don't be fooled. Behind the good-natured façade lurks the most cunning and logical brain in the entire kingdom. If there's a solution to your mystery, he's the only one who can find it."

"Let's not exaggerate, Charles," responded the visitor modestly. "But what mystery are you talking about?"

Jenny recounted again the harrowing details of her pursuit, but this time her manner was more assured. Charles Godley waited expectantly for a cynical smile to appear on his friend's lips, but in vain. On the contrary, his expression became more grave as the story proceeded. When she had finished, he remained silent for a while before asking a question.

"This 'golden ghost' of yours appears intermittently, doesn't it? Sometimes it's invisible; at other times it glows for a few seconds.'

Jenny's eyes opened wide in surprise.

"Why, yes! But how did you know? I don't think I mentioned that."

Unable to contain his admiration, Godley interrupted.

"Sickert is a veritable genius at deduction. I told you, Jenny, your mystery would yield to his faultless logic."

As if he hadn't heard this remark, his friend continued:

"I also assume that before you got here he followed you for a while in the nearby streets?"

Jenny's consternation was evident:

"But how in heaven's name—?"

"How did I know? Simple. I saw you."

"You saw her?" repeated Godley, in a strangled voice. "You saw her . . . and the ghost?"

"Yes," replied the other, solemnly and unequivocally.

"But that's not possible!" cried the host. "Not you, Sickert! You don't believe this twaddle?"

"Frankly, no. But I saw them as I was coming here, both her and the shining creature that was pursuing her. What I saw surprised me so much that I decided to walk around a bit before coming here. I told myself that I must have been dreaming, that it was my imagination, possibly stimulated by the approach of Christmas, that had been playing tricks. But what we have both just heard proves that wasn't the case."

"A shining creature," repeated Godley, more and more disconcerted, his eyes raised to the ceiling. "Explain it to me, Sickert, explain exactly what you saw."

His friend rubbed his chin.

"I was too far away to describe the scene precisely. But I can assure you that whatever it was glowed . . . and seemed to be made of golden reflections, just as this young woman has described." He turned towards Jenny. "Perhaps you didn't take proper note because you were fleeing the creature, Miss, but I was in a position to see its strange metamorphosis. At first, I didn't fully understand what was happening. I simply asked myself what caused you to run away like that. Then I saw it. It materialized behind your back for several seconds, then became invisible, then reappeared, then disappeared again, and so on."

"*But what did you see*, Sickert?" insisted Godley, clearly at the end of his tether.

"A thing . . . a luminous silhouette," confessed the other, with considerable embarrassment. "Its outline was golden, like a host of moving stars. I don't know how else to describe it."

"But that's not possible," insisted Godley. "Things like that don't exist! And in any case, the creature didn't leave any prints in the snow!"

"As far as I'm concerned, that doesn't prove anything," replied Sickert, "except that we're dealing with a phenomenon we don't understand."

There was another long silence. The visitor looked down in discomfort before the reproachful glare of his friend, who nonetheless offered him a glass of sherry. He accepted the first glass but not a second, for he had a business engagement that very evening which he had been unable to postpone. Shortly thereafter, he took his leave. Pausing at the door, he declared to a rather disappointed Godley:

"Next year, I promise, we'll spend the entire evening together. And I forgot to say how much I liked your Christmas tree. I congratulate you for the imaginative way you've decorated it."

Godley watched in frustration as his friend disappeared down the dark street, then closed the door and went to stand in front of his little tree. The decorations were certainly original, but the overall effect was miserable: the strips of crumpled paper were an expression of avarice rather than charity. He shrugged his shoulders and turned towards Jenny, silent and pensive in her armchair.

"So," he declared, "this whole incredible story is true after all. Now that I think about it, my friend's hasty departure could be because he's afraid. What do you think?"

"Maybe. But I'm more worried than he is, believe me!"

"Come now, you don't seem at all frightened at the moment."

"You don't think so? I'm so afraid . . . *He's* going to come back, don't you understand that?"

Godley cleared the lump in his throat, and asked:

"So, what should we do?"

"As I told you before: lock everything, barricade ourselves in as much as possible."

This time, Godley seemed to take her seriously and went about the task thoroughly. From one of the large boxes at the back of the room, he extracted some thick planks which he nailed across the closed shutters so solidly that it would have needed an axe to remove them. Even though the thick oak door had a large bolt, he also wrapped a chain around the latch and secured it with a padlock. That done, he returned to his seat, confidently announcing that they had nothing more to fear. The clock, striking the half-hour, answered in place of the girl, who appeared more and more nervous, as if the appearance of the ghost was now inescapable.

Jenny continued to stay silent while her eyes roamed anxiously over every corner of the room. Then, suddenly pointing to the hearth with a trembling finger, she cried:

"The chimney! There's still an opening!"

"Oh no, hardly," replied Godley with a nervous smile. "The last time I had it cleaned, the sweep got stuck inside, poor fellow. We had the devil of a job getting him out, even though he wasn't very big. He was about half your age and weight. Since then I've had a grill put in, because otherwise a small enough burglar could get in."

Jenny, however, wanted to check for herself. She used a poker to push the burning logs aside, then placed her pretty blonde head in the flue.

"That's not very smart," said Godley, disapprovingly. "You're going to scorch your hair. Look out! You've just dropped something in the fire."

"What?" asked Jenny, continuing her perilous inspection.

'A small object. I didn't have time to see it properly."

"I'd be surprised; I don't possess anything of value."

When she was once again settled in the armchair, her host observed, ominously:

"So here we are, Jenny: together and cut off from the rest of the world. One might say we're untouchable."

"So much the better."

"Do you really think so?" he asked, looking at her with strange amusement. "Didn't you have a strange impression when you were coming here?"

"Well, to be honest—"

"Like, for example, walking into the lion's den?"

There was a deathly silence, during which only the crackling of the fire could be heard. Suddenly Jenny, very pale, recoiled, staring at her host through eyes wide with fright as she stammered:

"The golden ghost. It's not you, is it? You don't even know me—you couldn't have any reason to want to hurt me!"

Charles Godley's smile froze menacingly on his face. Puffing out his chest, he declared:

"Oh, but I could. I could, for example, be that ignoble father who abandoned your mother on learning that she was pregnant. For, you see, I myself had to make a similarly hard decision in order not to disrupt my own career . . . Oh, yes! I could be that man and you could be my daughter, the child I never knew. I might, for fear of scandal, be obliged to reduce you to silence." He looked down at his huge, powerful hands. "And what better place than here, for from now on we are alone, cut off from the rest of the world."

"My God, I'm lost!" murmured Jenny, huddling in her armchair before emitting a shrill scream.

"Oh, you can always scream. We're quite alone. Alone in this room and, to all intents and purposes, alone in this street. So go ahead and scream!"

Then, with an abrupt change of expression, Godley threw his head back and roared with laughter. Almost choking, he spluttered:

"Please excuse me, Jenny. Forgive me for this jest, which was in bad taste. But seeing you sitting there so frail, so meek, so anxious, I was unable to resist. Really, I don't know what's come over me this evening, for I'm not normally like this at all. It's been years since I laughed so much. It must have been the sherry. Yes, look, the bottle's almost empty. Really, what an astonishing evening."

"Well then," replied Jenny in a hoarse voice, "please serve me the rest, for you've just given me a tremendous shock."

She offered her glass and downed the drink in a single gulp. Her big blue eyes misted over as she stared at her host, who continued:

"The truth is that I really was obliged to abandon a young woman I loved. The memory of her haunts me to this day, but I believe I've been punished, for I realised tonight that I've never known happiness. By that I mean I've never had a family or a warm hearth; never known a real Christmas."

"No happy Christmas, no family," murmured Jenny, lost in her dreams.

Godley placed a fatherly hand on his visitor's arm and sighed.

"We're each of us orphans in our own way."

"You're right, sir."

"I gave you a great fright, didn't I?" he asked in a voice full of emotion. "Well, I'll make it up to you, Jenny. I'm going to give you a Christmas present, a real Christmas present, a marvelous Christmas present."

"Oh, Mr. Godley, it doesn't matter."

"I insist. From now on, Jenny, you will be very rich. I'm going to leave you part of my fortune, which will allow you to live without a care for the rest of your days."

"You—you're teasing me."

"Not at all. I'm a very rich man, in spite of appearances. If you imagine every book and every file her corresponding to a furnished room, you'll get some idea of the size of my fortune."

"Oh, my goodness!" she exclaimed, looking all around. "It's incredible. It's marvelous!"

The ecstatic light in her eyes extinguished suddenly, and she added in a solemn voice:

"But, unfortunately, it's too late."

"Too late?" echoed the merchant. "But why, for God's sake?"

"Because it is I who will give you a present, Mr. Godley. A wonderful present. I'm going to give you a real Christmas celebration, a real warm hearth, just like the ones we never had but always dreamed about.'

"Really," said Godley, more and more intrigued. "And how are you going to do that?'

"Thanks to the golden ghost."

In the astonished silence which followed, her host looked with alarm at the locked and bolted door.

"Yes, he will come—despite all our precautions," continued Jenny in a strangely calm voice.

"But that's not possible! Nobody can get in! We're as safe here as in a strong-room."

"Nothing can stop the golden ghost."

"How can you be so sure?"

"Because I know his secret."

"But you told me—"

"Listen to me," interrupted Jenny, without losing her calm assurance. "His secret is easy to understand if you pay attention. I'm going to show you how your friend allowed himself to be fooled by a really simple trick."

The visitor got up, collected her bag, walked to the centre of the room, and said to her host:

"Watch carefully and follow my movements closely. I open several box-es, I take the matches and I gather them into small packets, like this . . . Are you with me?"

Godley, dumbstruck, could only nod his head.

"So I have my little packets of matches in hand, aligned so the sulphur heads are all in the same direction, so I just have to rub them to light them all at once, just as I'm doing now . . . Like this! Now I throw them into the air behind me and they fall in a shower of stars. Then I start again, and then a third time . . . Like this!"

"Obviously, you have to imagine the scene in the dark of night, in an alley, while I'm running as if I was scared to death and keep turning round as if the golden showers were the enemy on my heels. Outside, of course, the 'golden ghost' only shines for a few seconds, snuffed out by the snow. But here inside, he continues to live, fed by those ledgers which have caused so much heartache, by your files, by your boxes, by the paper garlands on your miserable tree, and soon by your entire office."

As if hypnotized by the young woman's fairylike demonstration, as she provoked showers of light by dispersing flaming matches to the four corners of the room, Godley reacted slowly. He made the error of panicking, of trying to extinguish all at once the myriad little fires which were lighting up the room like a forest of candles. As he rushed about in all directions, wild-eyed and haggard, he only half-listened to the explanations offered by Jenny, strangely radiant in the middle of the nascent fires.

"I knew that your friend came here every year at this time, when the streets are empty. My little drama astonished him, but everything made sense once he found me here and heard my story. So the golden ghost became a reality in his mind, to the point that he was able to give a completely misleading description when you asked him."

"Help me!" Godley shouted, his face crimson and dripping with perspiration. "We're going to be roasted like chestnuts because of your stupid farce. Unless you're completely mad—"

"Mad, undoubtedly, but it's because of you."

Godley shot her a murderous look, his hands reaching out as if to strangle her, but contented himself with pushing her aside. Every second counted. When he realised that it would be impossible for him to extinguish all the dispersed and growing flames, he headed for the door.

Jenny smiled mockingly as she watched him grappling in vain with the padlock and chain. A stifling heat permeated the office whose ceiling was gradually disappearing under a thick black cloud.

"The key!" screamed Godley. "You've hidden it, haven't you? Where is it?"

"Over there," chuckled Jenny, indicating the hearth. "That's what you saw falling into the fire just now."

Her host ran to the fire and tried to pull the logs away, first with the poker and then with his hands, but the flaming Christmas tree which fell across the grate hindered his efforts. When he was unable to stop coughing, and the thick smoke stung his eyes so severely that he could not keep them open, he concluded that it was a lost cause. He ran to the window and tried to open the shutters that he had so energetically nailed shut, without success. The blows he rained down with his bloody fists only succeeded in shaking the casements. When he finally stopped he could hear, over the roar of the fire, the distant sound of the church clock striking midnight.

Christmas? No, it was a frightful nightmare.

"Why?" he screamed, turning towards the visitor who continued to smile despite an almost incessant cough.

To Godley's eyes, standing as he was behind a curtain of fire, it seemed as if she were being consumed by the flames. Yet her voice remained mocking and curiously happy.

"You guessed it yourself, Mr. Godley. I am she whom you abandoned with her mother. She died as much from shame as from sickness. Since her death I have lived in the hope of finding you one day. I worked hard to pay for a private detective. But, once I found you, the most difficult thing was to channel my hatred and restrain the golden ghost, that demon of vengeance burning inside me, can you understand that? I needed to follow my plan patiently until the moment of our reunion."

Almost suffocated by the smoke, Godley could only dimly perceive the flaming silhouette in front of him. Nevertheless, it seemed to him that he could discern a beatific expression on her face before she added, amidst one final coughing fit:

"You see? I didn't lie to you. *He* did indeed come . . . The golden demon . . . The golden ghost. He's here, all around us, and more brilliant than ever. And at last we've found the warm hearth we've both been looking for . . . . "

THE TUNNEL OF DEATH

"You seem very thoughtful, sir."

Roussel turned and studied the man who had just spoken to him and was approaching him with a friendly smile. There was undoubtedly something elegant about the fifty-year old with the long, carefully groomed hair; but his clothes had seen better days, and he held his arm in a sling. Roussel had already made his diagnosis: one of those brave unfortunates that a stroke of fate had thrown on the street, struggling to maintain a vestige of dignity, and more in need of human contact than money.

Roussel offered a brief smile before answering:

"Thoughtful? Hard to be otherwise, with a tunnel that kept killing people."

For a few seconds, not a sound could be heard on that bleak October evening except the moaning of the wind blowing through Montmorency Street, in Le Havre.

"A tunnel?" gasped the newcomer, wide-eyed. "A tunnel killing people? Which tunnel?"

"Why, the tunnel which houses the escalator there," replied Roussel absent-mindedly, staring in front of him through the wire mesh fence which protected a short passage open to the sky, leading to a wooden door.

"An escalator? Ah, yes! That's what it says above the door."

"The biggest in Europe, nearly two hundred metres long. Thanks to this monster, it only took five minutes to reach the top of the town, otherwise . . . You're not from this region, are you?"

"No . . . No, I'm not from around here."

So saying, the man lowered his eyes. He was standing in front of the mesh fence next to Roussel, who inspected him discreetly, but not without a measure of sympathy. Evidently someone more used to sleeping under the stars than in a bed. Roussel was on the point of asking him how he had injured his arm, but held back.

"When you say this escalator has killed people," the man continued, now looking at Roussel with eyes of a strikingly clear blue, "I assume you mean there have been accidents?"

"No, not accidents. The escalator has killed three people, from revolver shots."

"From revolver shots? You must be joking! An escalator couldn't—"

"When it has been established beyond doubt that no human being could have done it, there is no other conclusion possible. Old Django warned us, by the way. He kept telling us: 'Don't shut down the escalator, don't do it. It will take its revenge, you'll see.' Nobody listened to him. Three people are dead, in circumstances which, as I said before, preclude any possibility of human involvement. An insoluble mystery, which has haunted me for years and which, every so often, brings me here at night. I stand here, in front of the fence, and I try to find an explanation. But maybe I should start at the beginning, if you're interested?"

"Very much so. But I must warn you, I'm a sceptic by nature. I don't really believe in haunted castles or other such places."

"You'll see, the facts tell it all. Several years ago, it was deemed preferable to put this escalator out of service because the funds couldn't cover the running costs. The municipal authorities set a date to shut it down, without taking into account the resentment of the people that used it, nor the warnings of old Django, a local gipsy and soothsayer. As I told you, he warned the municipal council members, buttonholing them in the street, telling them that the escalator would take its revenge if they insisted on closing it. The first murder took place the same week that the decision was announced, just at the time that people were returning home from work. In other words, at rush hour. There was the sound of a shot and a man in the middle of the escalator fell down, a bullet between his eyes. None of the people present had seen anyone pull out a weapon or make a suspicious movement. Which is pretty strange, you have to admit. There the people are, in single file on the moving stairs taking them to their destination, in a concrete tunnel offering no place to hide, each with eyes fixed on the person ahead. Nobody sees anything, and yet one of them is shot dead, right in the middle of the escalator. A few days later, the same scenario: a new victim in almost identical circumstances."

The stranger nodded his head, a smile playing on his lips:

"It's certainly strange, but an insoluble mystery? Maybe not. A lapse of concentration and someone could very well have . . . "

"I admit that. But now listen to what happened next. Shortly after the second murder, old Django alerted Bertrand Charpie, a rich industrialist of the region and one of the country's wealthiest men, and told him that he would suffer the same fate as the two others if ever he decided to take the escalator. Needless to say, Charpie hardly ever used that means of transport, but he was the type of man who could not resist a challenge—quite the contrary! That was how he had acquired his reputation and made his fortune. And so the day before the escalator was due to be shut down, Bertrand Charpie, in defiance of the prophecy, turned up . . . here, in fact, where we are standing right now.

"It was a grey September afternoon, and there had been several showers that morning. Charpie arrived with his wife, probably to underline his unswerving disregard for danger. Even so, he was accompanied by his bodyguard Martin, an ex-policeman, and by Pierre Picard, his young brother-in-law, a past master of martial arts. The police were also there. Needless to say, the escalator had been searched with a fine-tooth comb, and two officers had been posted here to guard the entrance, with two others at the exit.

"Imagine a seemingly endless concrete tube, three metres wide and almost two hundred long, dimly lit, with wooden steps about a square metre in size, slightly wider than deep. How could anyone hide in there?

"It was about three o'clock when Bertrand Charpie stepped on the escalator, with his wife, his brother-in-law, his bodyguard, and two inspectors. Obviously, then, there was therefore nobody on the moving steps apart from those six people, divided into three groups: Pierre Picard and one of the inspectors on the same step, ten metres ahead of Charpie and his wife, also side by side; then, ten metres behind them, Martin and the other inspector. It was in mid-journey that the shot rang out: a terrifying noise, in that tunnel, and with an echo every bit as frightening. Bertrand Charpie collapsed, mortally wounded by a bullet in the chest. He died that evening. Now can you see the problem?"

"Perhaps there was a hidden passage, or some opening that would allow the killer to fire a shot?"

"Nothing like that. As you can well imagine, after a crime like that the police examined every square millimetre with a magnifying glass. Furthermore, remember that the entrance and exit were being watched by police officers. They were adamant that, except for those accompanying Charpie, nobody left the tunnel after the murder; and prior to that, there wasn't even so much as a cat inside. The weapon was found on the side of the escalator, between the wall and the handrail, level with the spot where Charpie fell. A Browning 7.65, with no fingerprints."

The stranger shrugged his shoulders:

"So the killer can only be one of the five people who were with the victim."

"I was expecting you'd say that. First of all, please understand that the shot wasn't point-blank. The experts put it at a minimum of five metres. Which rules out Charpie's wife. In any case, the other four people were watching the couple closely and were ready to swear that there was no suspicious movement on her part at the moment the shot was fired. As for Martin and the police officer with him, standing ten metres behind the couple, each is ready to swear that the other could not have fired without being noticed. The same is true for the two people in front of the Charpies on the escalator. And I am particularly well placed to assure you that Pierre Picard could not have fired on his father-in-law. He was as close to me then as you are now. I could see his hands; with the one, he was stroking his chin, and with the other he was holding his raincoat against his chest, a little bit like . . . ."

The stranger looked at his arm in the sling with some amusement.

"Please excuse me," said Roussel. "I wasn't—"

"That's alright. No offence taken. If I've understood you correctly, you were the inspector next to him."

Roussel nodded.

"So you saw the murder committed before your very eyes?"

"Precisely. Picard and I were standing facing backwards, as we didn't want to lose sight of Charpie for an instant. We were literally petrified by the sound of the shot, and watched him clutch his chest before collapsing. His wife started to scream . . . It was difficult to determine the angle of fire because Charpie had just turned—or was still turning—at the moment the shot was fired. It was hard for us to work it out, and we weren't helped by the extraordinary effect of the echo. According to Madame Charpie, the shot had been fired right next to her. To me, the sound seemed to have come from several places at once."

"Seen from that point of view, things look pretty strange, I have to agree. But tell me, apart from the weapon, did you find any other clues?"

"Nothing, apart from cigarette ends and scraps of paper. No, wait, there was one object that did intrigue us. We found it next to the exit, on the side of the escalator: a piece of wood with a leather strap at the end. Nobody could work out what it was. In any case, the murder could not have been committed with it."

Roussel stopped, intrigued by the gleam of amusement in the stranger's eye.

"Life is made of coincidences," he observed, with a sort of dreamy contentment. "On the one hand, you're a flatf—detective. And now this strange object. It's incredible . . . . "

"Don't try and tell me that stick has something to do with the murder. I warn you, if you're thinking that it's some kind of ultra-sophisticated firing mechanism, you can forget about it. The experts were quite clear on that point."

"I never said that."

A long silence followed his words. Roussel had the distinct impression that the stranger had just solved the mystery. His calm and slightly condescending expression seemed to confirm that.

"From what I understand," he said, eventually, "the victim had a very forceful personality."

"Yes, indeed," agreed Roussel. "Bertrand Charpie was not at all your typical captain of industry. His audacity was legendary, he launched an extraordinary number of new endeavours, and always successfully. He had also made a very promising start in politics. Yet, despite all that, he remained a very simple man of the people. He could often be seen buying one of his workers a drink . . . . "

" . . . The more to exploit him. I see. I suppose that he also made grandiose philosophical speeches, preaching the love of one's neighbour and disdaining all base material things, such as money and property."

"Yes, he—"

"Do you honestly believe that it is possible to succeed as he did, by following the philosophy that he preached?"

"Well, I—"

"Wasn't he really the worst kind of hypocrite?"

"Maybe," replied Roussel, noncommittally. "But what's your point?"

"Just this: almost anybody could have held a grudge against such an individual, not least his relatives."

"That may be. But it's not the motive that's the problem, it's how the killer managed to do it. And I get the feeling,"added Roussel, his eyes narrowing, "that you have an idea."

"Idea?" said the stranger, with a smirk. "I'd say I was certain."

He stopped, looked furtively about him, thought for a moment, then continued:

"Listen, I can't tell you how it was done right now, but I'm sure you'll understand everything a few minutes after I've gone. For the time being, I'll give you a clue. The killer is obviously one of the people in the tunnel at the time of the murder. Someone who has been carrying out a diabolical plan: sacrificing two innocent people so that Charpie's death would look like some kind of curse. And I'll bet the old gypsy's palm was crossed with silver so he would utter his dire warnings. The challenge to Charpie was also part of the scheme: being the boastful braggart he was, he couldn't have ignored it without damaging his reputation. As to how the trick was worked, I think the killer threw an exploding cigar which he had just lit, an instant before he drew his gun, so as to create a diversion. I have to go now but, believe me, the rest will become clear to you. I'm sure of it."

Taken by surprise, Roussel watched the stranger vanish into the night. Only the flutter of a few dead leaves marked the spot where he had been standing just a moment before.

I can't tell you how it was done right now, but I'm sure you'll understand everything . . . a few minutes after I've gone.

Mad as a hatter, thought Roussel. Not only had he tried to pretend that he had succeeded where a professional like himself, Roussel, had failed over the years, but, to cap it all, he had claimed that the solution would become clear in a few minutes, as if by magic. A candidate for the loony bin, no doubt about it.

Roussel started back towards his flat, but sleep was out of the question. He ducked into a bar, ordered a double scotch, and looked at his watch: eleven o'clock. Fifteen minutes had gone by since the stranger had disappeared. He shrugged his shoulders, emptied his glass, and ordered another one. In his mind's eye, he saw the stranger with his arm in a sling. A curious individual. A tramp, as he had first thought? His eyes had been clear, not those of a wandering drunkard. Alert and mischievous . . . .

Ten minutes later, he decided it was time to head home. He called for the bill and reached in his pocket, only to find his wallet had gone.

His wallet, which had contained more than half his pay.

Not only had it gone, but there was a large hole in his pocket, cut cleanly, as if by a razor.

"Listen, Roussel," said the detective superintendent, trying to remain calm. "You've got a good many years left before you retire, and probably a couple of promotions. So, if I were you, I wouldn't go stirring up old cases which neither you nor anyone—"

"Picard threw the fake cigar away just before Charpie fell, I'm absolutely certain of it. He threw it to the side, and it exploded just as the Charpies drew level with it. He was waiting for the explosion and fired on Charpie the same instant. We took the two almost simultaneous explosions as an echo. Besides, do you remember there were different witness accounts about the direction of the shot?"

"O.K., O.K. Suppose that's true. How do explain that you didn't see him fire, even though he was only standing a few centimetres from you?"

Roussel opened a bag and pulled out a wooden rod about thirty centimetres long, with a short, wide leather belt attached at one end.

"This isn't the actual object that was found at the scene of the crime, but it's very much like it. Now, tighten the belt around my biceps, so that the rod crosses my chest horizontally. There, that's good. Now, take one of the gloves in the bag and the raincoat to hide the rod completely."

"A false arm," murmured the superintendent, in utter astonishment.

"Yes, a false arm. An old pickpocket's trick. There's also a false plaster arm and a false arm in a sling, but they don't concern us here. It's a perfect illusion, isn't it? It really looks as though the raincoat is on my arm, but my real forearm is free, behind my back. I remember Picard was wearing gloves. He was standing just as I am in front of you: almost facing me, but slightly turned so as to observe Charpie. And he simply fired on him with the hand behind his back. Granted it's not everyone who could aim accurately in those circumstances, but easy for an experienced marksman. And I recalled that he was a combat sports enthusiast."

"Hell's bells, Roussel, you've almost got me convinced. But, tell me, how did you tumble to the answer?"

"You probably know that I often used to walk around near the escalator after it was shut down. Thinking calmly, soaking in the atmosphere of the crime scene . . . "

Looking down, and fingering the stitched-up jacket pocket, Roussel said:

"One of these days, it was bound to . . . pay off."

THE CLEAVER

That evening, Owen Burns was in a particularly foul mood. The poor coach-man whose hackney cab took us to the *Hades Club* was the first to feel the brunt of it. My friend chastised him severely, merely because the poor fellow wore a waistcoat that didn't match his jacket!

"Lack of taste is worse than a crime, don't you know!" he expounded to his unhappy audience as he paid him for the trip. "Don't ever think of doing it again! I shan't hesitate to sue you for dereliction of beauty!"

A sudden cloudburst drenched Piccadilly Circus as we hastened to find the comfortable shelter of our favourite club. Once inside, we found our-selves seated next to a stocky individual who greeted us in a thick American accent. I feared for the worst, if only because my friend's bad temper had been caused by a lady who hailed from that same country. Throughout the whole afternoon, in fact, he had been ardently courting a singer from Texas who was on tour in London. A remarkably pretty young person, I must say, who unfortunately became bored with him after listening politely to his attempts at humorous banter. To his chagrin, she had left him abruptly and shortly thereafter had departed on the arm of a muscular cigar-smoking gentleman.

Even under the best of circumstances, my friend wouldn't have passed up the opportunity to scoff at one of our American cousins who, according to him, 'cultivated bad taste with a refinement hitherto unattained.' But this time, Owen surpassed himself. When we learned that our neighbour was on the staff of the United States embassy, I was convinced that we would not leave the club without having provoked a diplomatic incident.

He derided New World culture with a vengeance, culminating with his favorite anecdote about an American who ordered a copy of the Venus de Milo from a sculptor and was outraged when the merchandise was delivered missing two arms! The matter ended up in a court case, which he won.

"When all's said and done," Owen soliloquised in a deceptively playful manner, "I believe I know the reason for this basic flaw: these people have no history to speak of! That is, unless one excepts their fratricidal war."

By some miracle, our acquaintance turned out to be one of the most diplomatic people on the face of the earth. His polite smile and twinkling blue eyes did not betray any irritation or sensitivity, but simply an intrigued amusement. He must have asked himself what had got under the skin of this dandy with the affected airs and the fancy clothes, for him to behave in such a provocative manner.

"That's a grave charge to lay against the United States, sir," replied the American. "I'm sure that all the malcontents of our continent put together could not have come up with one like that! Forgive me if I don't entirely share your point of view."

"Don't mention it, my dear sir," said Owen, surprised and somewhat taken aback by the composure shown by our companion.

"As far as History with a capital H is concerned, yes, you are correct—we are a young nation," continued the American. "But as far as lurid local history, bizarre news items and weird cases, I can assure you we can hold our own with anyone."

"In short, your ghosts are as good as ours?" retorted Owen with a defiant gleam in his eye. "And you, Achilles, what do you think?" he added, turning to me.

"Er . . . I don't have an opinion in the matter," I replied cautiously.

The American went on to say that, although he was not an expert in the field, he knew of a number of strange and disturbing stories in which the phenomena reported defied all explanation. At this point I took the opportunity to introduce ourselves, emphasizing that I myself, Achilles Stock, and particularly Owen Burns were well experienced in this field. Even the experts at Scotland Yard had been known to call on the services of my friend when they encountered a particularly baffling case. Owen acknowledged my introduction:

"Modesty forbids me from mentioning that I've never been known to fail."

Our companion nodded thoughtfully, and then replied:

"Well, there are, nevertheless, mysterious cases which defy explanation.

I recall a murder case that was particularly disturbing, even though it was officially declared solved. The criminal was in fact arrested, but a number of aspects of the case remain unexplained to this day. And, despite your undoubted investigative talents, Mr. Burns, I doubt that even you could find a rational solution to the puzzle. If you wish, I can tell you the whole bizarre tale."

A gleam of interest came into Owen's eyes.

"I beg of you, sir. We're all ears."

"The events took place in the state of Colorado, dating back more than thirty years before, to the time shortly after the railroad reached the territory. It was, in fact, via this very means of transportation that Marcus Drake arrived in the town of Big Bridge one bright summer morning. It was not his final destination: the train was just making a short stop. Marcus was coming from Pikesburg, a town about a hundred miles to the east. He was planning to visit his friend, old Ben, who lived in String, the station just after Big Bridge. The town of String was perched on a hill overlooking a deep ravine which the railroad crossed via a spectacular wooden bridge, renowned for its stomach-churning effect on sensitive passengers! Old Ben was a dear friend, even though he had not seen him for quite a while. But on that particular day, Marcus had made a point of rising early in order to be in Pikesburg station in time to catch the train for String. He had an over-riding reason for seeing old Ben: he wanted to know if he was still alive!

For, truth be told, he had suffered a terrible nightmare several hours earlier: Old Ben was sleeping in a chair when a man approached him holding a meat cleaver. Marcus had seen his features quite clearly. In his dream he had cried out, in vain. The unknown man had raised the cleaver and dealt a tremendous blow to the sleeper's head. The force had been so great that the unfortunate victim had been thrown face down on the floor, and the cleaver had been so deeply embedded in the skull that the killer had been obliged to plant his foot on the victim's neck in order to pull it free. The nightmare had seemed so real, and so convincing, that Drake had woken up drenched in perspiration. It was then eight o'clock in the morning.

Three hours later, the thought of the dream still filled him with dread.

The sun was high in the sky and the compartment was becoming increasingly hot. Leaning against the frame of the window that he had just opened, he watched the handful of people waiting on the Big Bridge platform intently. Suddenly, he stiffened at the sight of one couple: a woman holding a small boy by the hand, and her strapping companion, a sinister-looking rosy-cheeked fellow, practically bald.

Stunned by what he saw, Marcus Drake held his breath: *the man was the spitting image of the murderer in his dream . . . .*

He shouted at the top of his voice, as the train slowed to a stop with axles screeching. The next moment, he was on the platform in front of the man, denouncing his abominable act in a loud accusatory voice, as a group of bystanders surrounded them. The words came out of his mouth in a torrent, yet he omitted no detail. The man remained silent, though evidently with great difficulty. He was twice the weight of the frail Marcus Drake and could obviously have flattened him with a single punch. However, his accuser appeared so sure of himself that he hesitated. The sheriff arrived at this juncture. Only a few minutes had gone by. The train had just left without Marcus, whose manner was becoming more and more aggressive, so much so that the sheriff had to intervene to calm him down. The matter was eventually discussed in his office.

The 'accused', one Harry Friedman, was well known in the town. A locksmith by profession, he spent most evenings in the saloon, winning or losing at poker. He was a violent individual, particularly when drunk, which was most of the time. Nevertheless, although he had been involved in numerous fights at the bar—mostly without consequence—he had never killed anyone. Until now, Harry Friedman may have been an ugly customer, but he was not a murderer. Furthermore, he vehemently denied the accusation and was outraged that the sheriff could give any credence whatsoever to the rantings of a stranger. How could anyone accuse him, Harry Friedman, upright citizen and model father? Hadn't he come to the station, together with his loved ones, to greet his elder son on his return?

Which was precisely the point that intrigued the sheriff. He wasn't used to such solicitude on the part of Friedman with regard to his family. Susanna, his wife, a pretty redhead, had a sad face which showed tired resignation. He wondered by what miracle she hadn't already left her brute of a husband, taking her two children with her. He had seen her several times with ashen features and a black eye, sometimes with facial bruises as well, the inevitable results of her husband's nocturnal visits to the saloon. They had two sons: Jonathan, the eight-year old who was with them at the station, and Peter, whose arrival the three of them had awaited in vain. Peter had just reached maturity and had found a position as shop assistant somewhere in a nearby town; he had long since failed to see eye to eye with his father. His occasional visits were strictly for the purpose of seeing his mother and brother.

Another thing that puzzled the sheriff was Friedman's hesitation when asked if he knew old Ben. It took a while before the locksmith admitted having met him on several occasions at the poker table. Given the charge leveled against him, his reluctance was understandable. Nevertheless, the sheriff found the whole business very strange, especially since Drake stuck steadfastly to his story. He swore he had never met Friedman, and *vice versa.*

It was after midday when the sheriff finally decided to pay a visit to old Ben. He called his deputy. Fifteen minutes later, the two men were in the saddle and on their way to String, the small town where the old hermit lived.

By rail, the journey took a half-hour, but the next train was not due at Big Bridge until late evening. At the halfway mark between there and String, the railroad track crossed the wooden bridge, but it was not possible to cross it on horseback. Thus the two lawmen had no choice but to take the steep and dusty road which wound round the hill. It was a long and difficult journey, particularly so because of the intense heat. The two horsemen arrived in String sometime around five o'clock in the afternoon, exhausted and with parched throats.

The temperature in the little town was like a furnace, and the streets were empty. A sinister foreboding gripped the sheriff on reaching old Ben's cabin. He couldn't get out of his mind the scene that had been so precisely described by Drake. A few moments later, there it was before his eyes: old Ben was there on the floor, his skull horribly split. Behind him lay an overturned chair and the murder weapon, the blade splattered with dark stains. The murder had been committed several hours before. The blood had dried, and the rigidity of the corpse left no doubt. However, on the neck of the victim they could clearly see a mark strongly resembling one that would have been left by the foot of the murderer when pulling the weapon free, exactly as foretold by their strange witness. The two men were stunned: *the incredible vision of Marcus Drake had come to pass in every detail!*

In the tiny adjoining kitchen they quickly discovered the motive for the crime: on the floor lay a wooden casket, smashed open. It had presumably contained old Ben's savings, for he was reputed to have hidden treasure on his premises ever since he had found gold in the mountains. He was, furthermore, a formidable poker player. Returning to the body, the two men noticed a shining object on the ground just underneath the dead man's right eye. It was one of those old dollar coins with a spread eagle on one side and a banner with the words 'E Pluribus Unum' inscribed on the other. But what intrigued the sheriff most of all was the condition of the coin. It had been severely damaged: half of the surface had caved in. A bitter smile spread across his dour features. He felt sure he recognized this coin . . . .

The following day in the late afternoon, the lawman, in the presence of his deputy, summoned Friedman to his office once again. This time, the interview was of an official nature. He had noticed Friedman shortly before midday with his family, including his older son who had just returned, but hadn't been taken in by their contented appearance, so different from normal. Meanwhile, the inquiry was making progress. By the side of a path leading to the old man's cabin, a blood-soaked shirt had been found, buried in haste and very recently.

Without further ado, the sheriff asked the locksmith if he recalled the time he had been challenged by a passing cowboy, who had fancied himself as a crack shot. He had claimed it was impossible to hit a dollar coin thrown in the air at a hundred feet. Friedman, much the worse for drink, had taken the bet and—no doubt with Bacchus's help—had amazingly hit it with his first shot. With some pride, the locksmith acknowledged the feat. He had scrupulously kept the coin, hiding it in the heel of one of his boots for good luck.

The three of them paid a visit to his house to inspect all his boots. However, he was unable to find the coin. He explained that, with the passage of time, it could have fallen out of the heel, which had been simply nailed to the sole. Besides, he wasn't even sure that he still had the boots in question. To Friedman's great surprise, the sheriff then produced the damaged coin. He went on to explain where he had found it, and how the killer, in the process of planting his foot savagely on the neck of the victim, must have lost it. The suspect, spluttering, was reluctant to claim ownership but his family confirmed it, as did some of his friends later on. From then on, the noose started to tighten. The doctor who examined the body placed the time of death between fairly wide limits, but definitely between dawn and the early afternoon. Old Ben could well have been killed at seven thirty in the morning, the moment at which Marcus Drake had his 'dream.' Friedman was unable to produce an alibi. Totally drunk, he had spent the night in a barn and did not turn up to see his family until mid-morning, around ten thirty. With a good horse, he could have come back from String in three hours. But the most damaging proof was without question the bloodstained shirt. His wife Susanna identified it by the sleeve, which she had repaired in two places.

The loot from the attack on old Ben was never found. But it was soon revealed that he and Friedman had frequently got into arguments at the poker table over disputed games, which the loser had taken particularly badly. No alibi, a motive, and two damning pieces of evidence: for Friedman the die had been cast.

When the sheriff had first heard Marcus's story, he had almost laughed in his face. He had only listened so as to try to calm him down. After all, how could anybody be accused of murder because of a dream? No prosecutor would have agreed to convene a jury! Nevertheless, the one which gave its verdict two weeks later had no hesitation at all. They briefly considered the possibility of Drake having concocted a scheme against the accused, but that was dropped when it was shown that the two men were previously unaware of each other's existence. Furthermore, Marcus Drake had lived a blameless life up to that point. The bank where he worked had hired him because of his integrity. And he had an unshakable alibi, several witnesses having seen him at the station on the morning of the crime. Finally, and above all, if he had indeed been implicated in the murder of old Ben, it would have been insane for him to act the way he did, namely to describe his incredible nightmare vision. And he confirmed not having said a word to anyone about it until he saw the murderer standing on the platform of Big Bridge station.

Unable—for obvious reasons—to explain his 'dream,' he was nevertheless commended by the jury for his intervention, in all likelihood due to divine providence. Thanks to him, the hand of justice had fallen on a particularly odious individual. And Harry Friedman was hung high the following week."

The American stopped his narrative, lit a cigar languidly, looked calmly at his drinking companion, and asked:

"So, Mr. Burns, what do you think?"

"The affair seems quite clear to me as far as—"

"Excuse me?" spluttered the American, eyes wide in amazement. "Do you mean to say you can explain the vision in rational terms?"

"Yes. Or at least in terms more rational than in your account, remarkably accurate though it was. But am I right in assuming you yourself were directly involved in this affair as a witness? You might even be little Jonathan, judging by your apparent age. For that matter, my dear sir, we don't actually know your name."

The American nodded his head and, smilingly, admitted:

"You're quite right, I am in fact Jonathan Friedman. No doubt I was too young at the time to be deeply marked by what happened, but I was affected by the events nevertheless . . . That damning 'vision' has remained a mystery to me ever since, which is why I have difficulty believing what you say. Sincerely, if you can truly explain what happened, I am prepared to give you—"

Owen raised a hand magnanimously.

"No, I don't want anything, my dear fellow. I am an aesthete: I only work for the love of my art. But for now, I will hand things over to my friend Achilles Stock. Like you, he is a man accustomed to the open sky and wide open spaces. He was brought up in South Africa. His is a sound mind in a sound body, and he should thus be expected to come to the same conclusions as myself."

I took up the thread, clearing my throat while secretly cursing my friend. I was convinced he was bluffing and playing for time, for this puzzle appeared to be completely insoluble. I attempted to follow to the letter those methods of reasoning that he claimed were so dear to him.

"There are two possibilities and only two," I started, somewhat pedantically. "The first possibility is that it was a genuine premonition. If that is indeed the case, there is nothing further to add. The second possibility assumes the complicity of Marcus Drake, however honorable he may appear to be. It has to be one or the other, there's no getting away from it. If Drake is guilty, he could have acted with an accomplice and hired a contract killer to take care of matters while he acted out his little game."

"No, Achilles," interrupted Owen, in a professorial tone. "Our friend pointed out quite rightly that such behavior would have been completely out of character for a bank employee. He would have attracted all kinds of suspicion. In those days, that meant being hung high and dry. It would have been much too risky."

"Do you know what happened to the fellow?" I asked Jonathan Friedman. "Didn't he try to woo your mother afterwards?"

The American shook his head.

"No. We never saw him again. My mother did remarry shortly afterwards, but not to him. The sheriff handed in his badge in order to devote himself entirely to ensuring her happiness."

I felt a growing suspicion. But Jonathan Friedman read my thoughts. With a soothing gesture, he assured me:

"I had the same idea as you, Mr. Stock, but my stepfather could not have been the murderer. It was physically impossible. He had several visitors in his office throughout the morning of the crime. It would have been impossible to ride to String on horseback and get back in time, taking into account the time of the murder. And there were no trains during that period of the day. Shame, isn't it?" he added with a wry smile. "He would have made an excellent culprit, I agree!"

"Yes, because he could have bribed Marcus Drake to fabricate the whole story."

"No, no, Achilles," interrupted Owen with some irritation. "I keep telling you that theory doesn't hold water. Too dangerous! If Drake had spilled the beans they would both have found themselves in deep trouble."

"So, if we rule out the dream as a sort of premonition, the only theory left is some form of suggestion. The murderer somehow put the vision of the crime into Drake's head."

"And how, pray, did he do that?"

"Through hypnosis."

'Hypnosis?" sniffed Owen Burns, looking at me almost with disdain.

"Do you really want us to believe that by using such a method, someone could have planted a dream as precise as that in his head? Really, Achilles, you disappoint me! Such silliness is not worthy of you!"

"So," I said, throwing my arms up in exasperation, "then we must accept that it was a premonition pure and simple! I tell you, it has to be one or the other, it can't be anything else!"

In the next moment, Owen found us both looking at him. We awaited his explanation. I found myself wondering how he was going to get out of it, and I wouldn't have changed places with him for anything. It was obvious that the tension was pressing heavily on our companion, to his considerable discomfort. He could not get away with a glib response. Two setbacks from Americans in a single day would leave an indelible mark on his self-respect. But, as always, he managed to surprise his audience, by simply replying:

"No."

There was a heavy silence at our table; in the confined atmosphere of the club, the conversations at the adjacent tables could be heard more clearly.

"No," he repeated. "There is another possibility. Not that I am criticizing you, Achilles. Your reasoning was sound, but you ruled out some theories too hastily, so that in the end you overlooked the only valid possibility. Before giving you my personal opinion on the matter, I would like simply to pose a question to our friend. Mr. Friedman, could you tell us what happened to the principal players?"

"Yes, of course. In fact, very few of them are still alive today, except maybe that strange Marcus Drake. Peter, my elder brother, took to the bottle like my father and ended up taking his own life. My mother never got over that last tragedy and died the following year. My stepfather died quite recently."

"At the time, did anyone regret the passing of your real father?"

Jonathan Friedman gave a deep sigh.

"No, not really. It was actually a great relief. Compared with the life she was living with that man, hell would have been preferable for my mother. I've tried to wipe certain painful scenes from my memory, when he beat her violently after bouts of drinking, but such things are not easily forgotten."

Owen nodded his head:

"That's what I thought. It's obvious that we're dealing with an avenging killer, whose mission was to eliminate your father."

"But who?" exclaimed Friedman.

"The only person who could have physically committed the crime and placed the 'proof' at the right moment. What protected him so well was precisely that 'vision' of Drake's, plus the especially favorable circumstances. It was an opportunistic crime of the highest quality, demanding an exceptional degree of intelligence and nerve. However, properly executed, it left its perpetrator every chance of escaping justice. You see, Achilles, your big mistake was not envisioning *all* the possible solutions. There was a third one: that Drake's 'vision' was just that: a dream pure and simple, and our cunning murderer exploited it to the full, *after the event*."

"After the event?" I exclaimed in astonishment. "But at what point did the killer learn of the famous 'dream'? Drake hadn't spoken to anyone before he saw Harry Friedman on the platform at Big Bridge, around eleven in the morning. And by that time the crime had already been committed!"

"No, the latest time for the crime was the early afternoon. Let's say midday. Let me remind you that it was during the few minutes that the train was in the station that Drake described his dream, accusing Friedman in front of anyone who wanted to hear. If the murderer had been present at that moment, and had realized what a great opportunity it was to dispose of Friedman, he would have had an hour to do the job. That is to say: killing old Ben and planting a couple of damning clues at the scene of the crime."

"But it takes a good three hours to get to String!"

"On horseback, yes. But by train it only takes half an hour . . . . "

"I understand!" interjected the American. "The killer was in the train! He observed the scene playing out on the station platform, and stayed in the compartment so as to descend at String."

"Exactly," said Owen. "Then all he had to do was to take old Ben's cleaver, kill him exactly as the 'visionary' described, and then plant the two 'clues'."

"But how could he have had the clues to hand, since he had been more or less obliged to improvise the whole thing?"

"A very good question, Mr. Friedman. And one which answers itself . . . Who could have had in his suitcase, or even on his feet, a pair of boots belonging to your father; know that the famous coin was in the heel; and possess a shirt that had been repaired by your mother? Who nurtured such a deep hatred of your father that sacrificing old Ben would not have deterred him? I can only see one person satisfying all those conditions. It's even been confirmed that he was traveling by train that very day."

The American clutched his forehead suddenly with both hands:

"My God! Peter . . . "

There was a silence, during which Owen slowly nodded his approval:

"To be sure, that does not explain why Drake had his nightmare when he did. But nightmares, horrible though they may be, are fairly common events, are they not? In any case, it seems to me that our version of the story is the most plausible. What do you think, my dear sir?"

In a strangled voice, Jonathan Friedman declared:

"Now I understand why he suddenly started drinking heavily. What do I think? I think, Mr. Burns, that you have been absolutely brilliant. One would almost think you were American!"

THE FLOWER GIRL

In that December evening of 1903, London was shivering under a fresh fall of snow. A white cotton-wool blanket froze the capital in a strange serenity; it tempered the city's feverish activity, deadened the noise of the hackney cabs' iron wheels, and muffled the holly sellers' shouts to the passers-by. The chiming of the bells was but a faint and distant chorus, and even Big Ben, which was then sounding five o'clock, seemed more subdued than usual. Dark clouds hung over the city. It was almost dark, and already the gas lamps were gleaming the length of the Strand. Despite the approach of the Christmas season, it was a cold, sad, and gloomy day, which mirrored our own mood only too well.

Behaegel and I were taking tea with my friend Owen Burns. We had been carousing into the early hours and nobody felt like talking. The tall and debonair Owen was at that moment a mere shadow of his normal self. Standing morosely at the window, his hands behind his back, he watched the street below. Art critic by profession—even though he excelled in other areas, such as criminal detection—he cultivated eccentricity as an art form, and had few equals for drawing attention to himself and, wherever possible, causing scandal as if his honour depended on it. In fact, as recently as the night before, at a preview for a forthcoming art exhibition, he had once again run true to form.

He had been asked to assess the talent of the painter, a young Spaniard of solemn and haughty demeanour, a friend of the royal family. His response: 'ugliness defined as fine art' had made some of the journalists laugh, but had been less appreciated by the other guests. The artist, livid, could hardly contain himself. In a steely voice, he had asked that Owen leave the gallery, to which my friend replied that he had no right, on English soil, to make such a demand. A diplomatic incident had been avoided by a hair's breadth.

But the evening was not yet over. At dinner a little later, he found himself seated next to a slender, pretty blonde named Lydia. He launched into paeans of praise about her ethereal beauty, despite the presence of a seemingly pleasant and amiable fellow of some forty years—who was none other than her husband. When the man, during his wife's absence from the table, explained his role in the young woman's life, Owen had seemed stunned. For a moment we had thought that the fair Lydia's husband, who had contained himself thus far, would pounce on Owen and pound the living daylights out of him. But it was not to be. The fellow had burst out laughing, saying how amused he had been by Owen's remarks. He had even congratulated him on his brilliant patter, worthy of the colourful characters that he, Mickael Behaegel, playwright, created for a living. After that the two men got on famously, and the evening finished well after midnight on a happy note. We left the inn singing 'She'd never had her ticket punched before', and quite impervious to the cold, in large part due to the gallons of ale we had consumed.

Behaegel was slumped in a deep armchair next to the chimney, playing with the chain of his fob watch, quietly lost in thought, like Owen Burns himself. I myself was thinking about his wife and what a strange couple they made. Behaegel's complacency had been surprising, while the beautiful Lydia, she of the laughing eyes, had seemed to appreciate Owen's blatant flattery. Then, suddenly, she had got up and left. Owen's thoughts must have been running along the same lines, because at that moment he broke the silence:

"Your wife left quite suddenly last night. Was she taken ill?"

"No. She went back to the hotel to get some rest, because she has to take the boat back to the continent this morning. I shall be meeting her in two days, to pass Christmas together." He looked at his watch. "In fact, given the hour, she must be there already: she has a show tonight."

"She's in one of your plays, then?" asked Owen, intrigued.

"No, Lydia is a ballet dancer, in Paris."

Owen's face was a picture of surprise and admiration, as Behaegel explained that, the two of them being artists, they could not see each other as regularly as most couples. He himself divided his time between London and Paris. But, despite that, they were a very close couple, making up for their frequent separation with a discreet but profound complicity.

"A discreet but profound complicity," murmured Owen with an appreciative smile. "I understand."

From the depths of his armchair, Behaegel replied:

"It's well known, Burns, that an artist's life is not always an easy one!"

"Look who you're talking to, my dear fellow! I am better placed than anyone to know that, being myself the epitome of the aesthete!"

"You'll have to excuse me," said Behaegel, clearing his throat, "but last night I didn't quite catch what you do for a living. To hear your friends talk, you're an expert in everything!"

With a complacent smile, Owen raised his hand in mock self-deprecation:

"That's not an unfair portrait, I must admit in all modesty. But, by the very nature of things, I have tended to specialise in one particular area. Scotland Yard often takes advantage of my natural generosity, so I frequently give my humble point of view when our celebrated police come up against a problem too complex for them."

Our guest's face lit up:

"So you're a detective?"

"In a sense, yes. But I *only* involve myself with truly unusual cases, those beyond common understanding; or, if you will, crime in its most enigmatic and therefore most artistic form."

"I understand," replied Behaegel, with a curious look at his host.

Owen went quiet for a moment, contemplating the street below, then declared:

"What a sad yet inspiring tableau. I am always moved by the sight of beauty so pure."

"Do you speak of the winter landscape?" asked Behaegel.

"Snow possesses the infinite virtue of erasing the imperfections of the modern world. Its sparkling cloak softens the landscape, enhances the architecture, overcomes human baseness, and restores the faith of even the most demanding aesthetes such as myself. Its beneficial effect is undeniable. But I was thinking of something quite different. Come here, my dear friends. Look down there, at the corner of the street, at that ravishing creature of such pure beauty."

We joined our friend at the window. The 'beauty' in question was a flower seller who was holding a basket of dried flowers almost as big as herself. She must have been fifteen or sixteen years old. Shivering in a threadbare coat, she smiled wanly at the passers-by as she timidly offered her flowers. The fading light of the gas lamp fell on her frail silhouette, creating golden highlights in her blonde hair, like so many tiny candles. Her face, with its sunken cheeks, seemed very pale. She was without question a beautiful child, despite her thinness and the misery which permeated her whole being.

Accustomed as I was to such grandiloquent remarks from my friend, I offered my opinion in no uncertain terms.

"You don't understand, Achilles," replied Owen tersely. "Beauty is precisely the suffering of the soul. Look at that charming young face, as pure and natural as the snow, set apart by its dignity and grace from those self-styled Amazons that strut about in the park as if they own the place. And I'm talking about the prettier ones, because the others, even if they are striking, are far from beautiful!"

For several minutes, Owen gave vent to his own very personal and very demanding concept of art, before unexpectedly taking up the cause of the unfortunate poor, who were to be pitied more than ever at this time of year.

"They can't even afford a meal worthy of the name once a year!" he went on, continuing his harangue. "Not to mention those poor little children who can only stare hopelessly at the Christmas display of toys no Santa Claus will ever bring! And I'm sure the only company that poor girl, obviously forced to sell flowers in such weather, will have at Christmas will be a miserable candle in a chipped glass! No, really, life is too unfair!"

So saying, he donned his jacket, asked us to excuse him for a few minutes, and left the room. He returned a few minutes later, carrying the large basket of dried flowers which we had just seen in the arms of the young girl.

"I bought everything she had," he said, his face glowing with delight. "If you could have seen how she looked at me! The grateful surprise in her eyes! I wouldn't have missed it for anything! And that's not all, my friends: tomorrow I shall take her to see one of the greatest portrait painters in the country, so that he may immortalise that beautiful face. I know it will make a magnificent picture!"

Speaking for myself, I'm used to these kinds of outbursts from Owen, but Behaegel reacted differently. Seemingly lost in thought, he said nothing at all. When he eventually spoke, what he said seemed as strange as the behaviour of my friend.

"What a remarkable coincidence! The snow, the nearness of Christmas, and—most of all—the flower girl! It all seems like a fairy tale: like a fairy tale that really happened."

"Life *is* a fairy tale," said Owen.

Behaegel turned to him and asked, perfectly seriously:

"Do you believe in Father Christmas?"

Owen, taken by surprise, did not reply.

"The grown-ups don't believe in him any more, obviously," continued Behaegel, with a shrug of the shoulder. "And that's quite understandable. Nevertheless, gentlemen, I could tell you a story *which proves his existence beyond a shadow of doubt*, because what happened could quite simply not be explained otherwise. What's more, the circumstances were so extraordinary that when the police investigated the murder, they gave up trying to reconcile the various conflicting testimonies."

"You interest me strangely, my dear fellow," said Owen, stroking his chin. "Would this be an insoluble puzzle?"

Behaegel continued to stare at the fire dancing in the hearth. In the flickering illumination of the flames, his face seemed almost sculpted in bronze. He answered with an ironic smile:

"Insoluble, yes, because no-one could find an explanation for what would better be described as a 'miracle'."

Owen could not conceal his growing astonishment:

"A miracle? Isn't that something of an exaggeration?"

"No, I don't think so. How else to describe the extraordinary events, witnessed by a handful of people, which took place in a respectable London house just before Christmas a few years ago?"

"Even though he was extremely wealthy, old Drake Sterling lived frugally. His house was as cold as his heart, and as austere in appearance as he was himself. It was a vast Tudor-style mansion with a steeply sloping roof bristling with gables, whose silhouette loomed over a respectable part of London. Yet he hoarded lumps of coal. With the exception of his customers, he showed scant interest in his fellow beings, ostentatiously ignoring beggars and other poor devils. Pity and charity played no part in his thinking, solely preoccupied as he was with the smooth functioning of his business affairs.

"He owned a boutique in the heart of the city where the best fabrics could be found, coming not only from the British Isles, but also the conti- nent and countries of the Far East. Silky scarlet damasks, magnificent tur- quoise madras cottons, superb merinos, and other shimmering materials rustled under watchful, greedy eyes. The two young apprentices who served his customers were rarely idle. Until recently, they had been helped in their work by one Buckley, a salesman who had worked for Sterling for many years; but the rich merchant had fired him.

"Before that, poor Buckley had already been having a hard enough time making ends meet looking after his only child, Sidonie, and paying the rent—which was very high for his modest two-room flat in an imposing building not far from Sterling's house—his landlord being none other than Sterling himself. However, the rich merchant was reluctant to put Buckley and his daughter on the street, because his employee's condition after get- ting the sack was far too pitiful. Reduced to begging, Buckley had taken to the bottle and many felt sorry for poor little Sidonie who, although only twelve years old, was obliged to wander the cold wet streets selling her bou- quets of dried flowers, the only meagre income the family had.

"Previously, Buckley had been pleasant and amusing company with a strong sense of humour, whose presence enlivened the fabric shop and con- trasted with the dry and rigid personality of the proprietor. His dismissal had turned him into a wreck, a poignant and sad example of human de- cline. According to some, his boss had sacked him for 'economic reasons': in other words to save money. According to others, it had been a personal matter. It was Sterling himself who cleared the matter up, one Christmas Eve two years later.

"On such occasions, the rich merchant was in the habit of inviting his close relatives over. It was the only time he showed any sign of generosity. It's true that his circle of intimates was small. There was his sister Margaret, her husband John Hopper, their only child Theodore, and Ronald Ark, a fabric importer with his seven-year old son Tommy. Although the Hoppers spent a few days with their 'Uncle Drake' regularly at that time of year, Ron- ald Ark was there for the first time. According to some, this convivial fam- ily dinner was supposed to cement their business relationship. Ronald Ark, thin and dry, with an aquiline profile, resembled Sterling somewhat, except that he was in the prime of life. He wore a frock coat and an impeccable olive-coloured three-piece suit. The chain of the gold watch that decorated his waistcoat testified to his success. The master of the house, himself, was well past sixty. His hair was gray, and his back was hunched, perhaps from the weight of the years, but more likely from that of the fortune that he had amassed. And what, incidentally, was its value?

"The Hoppers could doubtless be counted among those asking that question. Margaret was a stout woman with rather plain features. Passivity appeared to be her dominant characteristic, except when she addressed her husband. Wrinkles of reproach creased her brow whenever she looked at him, as if she were perpetually rebuking him for not having succeeded like her brother. John, chubby and cheerful, smiled from the depths of his armchair, a glass of sherry clutched in his plump fingers. A model of discretion, he spoke little. He taught natural history in a London school and appeared content with his lot. Approaching their fifties, they seemed very different from their son, Theodore, who was only thirteen but had legs like stilts and was taller than either of them. His dreamy expression, his cherubic features, and his fascination with little Tommy, reflected an innocent nature that his parents seemed never to have possessed. The same was true of Tommy himself: it was hard to imagine that he might one day become a ruthless business man like his father. His face held the same delighted expression that all children of his age showed at the approach of Christmas. The golden lights of the candles and the sparkle of the crimson balls hanging on the Christmas tree beside the fireplace could be seen reflected in the eyes of the two children, wide with wonder.

"That year, Sterling had made a special effort to decorate the lounge. Holly branches and silk ribbons garnished the window frames, the doors, and the mantelpiece. The tree itself was much bigger than usual. Yet, the rich merchant had good reason to be in a bad mood. The week had started badly. The arrival of the Hopper family, and the resulting supply problems that created, had put him, and particularly his housekeeper, on edge as the brunt of the extra work fell on her. The following day, a fire—whose origin had as yet not been determined—had broken out in the laundry-room. Sterling, without the slightest proof, had accused the elderly servant of negligence. Luckily, the blaze had been quickly brought under control. Nothing remained of the clothes and sheets stacked in the room but, by some miracle, the fire had not spread to the adjoining shed where Sterling stored his most precious wares. The thought of having come so close to catastrophe had tempered his anger somewhat, and even inspired a spirit of generosity and jollity quite foreign to him.

"So, that year, there was a roaring fire in the lounge, the like of which had not been seen before. The dinner was equally exceptional. The large and succulent turkey had been much appreciated, as had the punch that had been served beforehand, and which had brought a glow to the adults' cheeks—including Drake Sterling's. After the meal, his judgment no doubt clouded by the wine, he held forth on the sad fate of the poor. It was assumed at first that he was motivated by compassion: that the sight of flakes of snow falling behind the steamed-up windows had softened his heart. But that was not the case.

"He spoke about Buckley. The gleam of satisfaction in his eyes made it obvious that he did not regret having dismissed his old salesman. That evening he made it clear that he had finally got rid of him because of his flippant manner, his incessant banter, and his general good humour, totally out of place in such a serious establishment. Furthermore, he had committed the unpardonable sin of making fun of Drake Sterling's parsimonious nature in front of several customers. It was too much. Sterling, intransigent, was unmoved by the pleading of his old employee. What about Sidonie? 'It was her father's problem, not mine. He had to accept his responsibilities.'

"In an instant, an icy silence fell on the gathering, and the ephemeral spirit of young Sidonie, pale and fragile, could be imagined crossing the room, carrying her large basket and covered in frost. A new round of drinks was quickly served at this juncture and, shortly before midnight, everyone went outside on the front porch to partake of the night air

"I must stop here to describe the layout of the premises, which is essential in view of the quite incredible events which were soon to happen. A path passed right in front of Drake Sterling's house, on the other side of which was a small river. The path itself was about four yards wide, and had to be crossed carefully, especially in winter, to avoid taking a bath in the freezing waters below. A warehouse with a high wall separated Sterling's house from that where Buckley and his daughter lived, the last house on the street, some fifteen yards away. Almost no-one except the Buckleys went there.

"Throughout the whole week, each fall of snow had been followed by a freeze. The white coat covering the capital was becoming thicker every day. It had been snowing since the beginning of the evening, so much so that Sterling and his guests could see nothing but a smooth white blanket covering the ground and the roofs, like a world covered in icing sugar. Only the river broke the white monotony, a dark ribbon in which were reflected the lighted windows on the opposite bank: splashes of yellow and purple bobbing on the cold surface. At that moment, the snow was falling lightly. The white coat, unbroken, glistened under the light from the two lamps on either side of the front entrance. There was not a mark on the path; nor in front of the steps; nor to the right towards the junction with the main highway; nor to the left towards the Buckley's house. To be truthful, nobody paid any particular attention at the time, but it was an indisputable fact. Everyone had looked to the left, because Tommy had asked if little Sidonie had received, as he and Theodore had, beautiful Christmas presents. They had both been particularly spoiled that year. Theodore had received a basket of oranges and dates, and a pair of woollen gloves. Tommy's heart had been sent racing by the sight of a gorgeous rocking-horse. Sterling replied tersely that Sidonie's presents depended on her father, or more precisely on his behaviour.

"As if to soften the hard edge of his comments, church bells started to ring out everywhere. The small gathering lingered a while to listen to the joyful sounds spreading throughout the city, then Sterling decided it was time to go back inside. He turned towards the door, followed by his guests, then—doubtless struck by conscience—gave one last look at the Buckley's house, which at that moment was shrouded in darkness.

"Ten minutes later, they were warming themselves in front of the fireplace, when suddenly the jingling of little bells could be heard outside. In surprise, Tommy shouted:

'It's Father Christmas! He's bringing presents!'

'He's already been, I think,' said Sterling, through clenched teeth.

The boy put a finger to his lips:

'Yes, that's true! So it must be for Sidonie. That's it, he's come back for Sidonie!'

'Impossible!' interrupted Sterling, irritated. 'There's no Father Christmas for Sidonie!'

'But there is! Can't you hear the reindeer bells?'

'Yes!' sneered Sterling. 'So look out of the window, before he goes away!'

Without waiting to be asked a second time, the little boy pressed his impish nose to the misted glass. As he raised his dreamy and ecstatic eyes to the sky, Sterling asked him, sarcastically:

'Well, did you see him?'

'Yes, of course,' replied Tommy after a short silence. 'He's coming out of Sidonie's house.'

Sterling winked at the child's father, and continued:

'So I assume he's getting back on his sleigh, pulled by reindeer?'

'Yes, he's just in front of the house. But he's leaving now. Oh! He's flying away.'

'That's quite natural, Tommy, it's Father Christmas. It's beautiful, isn't it? The sleigh flying towards the stars. But make the most of it, because soon you won't be able to see such things!'

'Why, Mr. Sterling?' replied Tommy, thoughtfully, as he pulled back from the window. 'I don't understand . . . .'

'You'll understand soon. My little Theodore already understands, because I explained it to him last year, didn't I, Theodore?'

Without saying a word, the beanpole solemnly nodded his head in agreement, but reluctantly, as if it was against his will.

Sterling, satisfied, proposed one last toast to his guests, then murmured dreamily:

'They're strange, all the same, those bells. The sound seemed too close to have come from the other side of the river. Now, I don't know who would amuse themselves by playing Father Christmas around here. There's nobody in the street but ourselves. Buckley? Impossible. He must be blind drunk at this hour!'

Nobody could answer the question, so they decided to look outside.

A quarter of an hour had gone by since their last time outside. It had almost stopped snowing: just a few flakes swirled in the sky. The path was still as quiet as a tomb, but someone or 'something' had left tracks in the snow. Particularly strange tracks, because they did not obey any of the laws of physics.

"From a point on the path half way between the two houses and ending at Buckley's door, the characteristic ruts of a sleigh and the prints of several large quadrupeds could be seen. *But they came from nowhere!* They appeared suddenly in the middle of the snow, continued for about ten yards, then disappeared mysteriously! It was absolutely incredible!

"What's more, they were fresh, for the witnesses were prepared to swear that there had been no prints there a quarter of an hour before. But their consternation knew no bounds when they got closer and realised that, over a relatively short distance of five or six yards, the ruts *became gradually deeper in the snow then shallower before vanishing completely!* As if a reindeer-drawn sleigh had come down from the sky, landing in the snow and gliding as far as Buckley's house, before taking off and flying away again!

"There were large footprints going to and fro between the Buckley front door and the spot where the sleigh appeared to have stopped.

'It's Father Christmas!' cried Tommy. 'He came to bring presents for poor Sidonie!'

"The Buckley house was no longer in darkness. The windows were lit up and, from the front door, which was slightly ajar, came a ray of light. Sterling, now in a panic, decided to knock. Not getting any response, he went in, followed by his guests.

"There were further surprises in store for the little group. A fire was burning in the grate. A fire at least the equal of Sterling's, and bright enough to illuminate the large room by itself. A magnificent Christmas tree stood near the hearth: at its feet a number of parcels wrapped in shining paper and tied with ribbons. A rocking-horse, brand new and larger than Tommy's, watched over the presents, its brilliant red colour contrasting starkly with the drabness of its surroundings. There was nobody in the room, or in the bedchamber next door. All the windows were closed, so the front door was the only way in.

"*So who, then, had lit the fire?* The mysterious stranger that had arrived by sleigh, that had left his footprints on the doorstep and brought so many presents? On the evidence, it could only have been him. Yet he had apparently come down from the sky, just like a fairy tale. It was beyond comprehension.

"Befuddled and bemused, the witnesses tried in vain to find an explanation for the incredible facts, while little Tommy clung to his father's knees, murmuring:

'It's Father Christmas, daddy. He's kind. He didn't forget Sidonie.'

"Sterling's face twitched. The situation seemed more and more absurd to him, and the remarks unwelcome and out of place. Angrily, he ordered the child to be quiet. Eyes blazing, he kept himself barely under control.

"It was at that moment that Sidonie burst into the room, her basket of dried flowers over her arm. It was still almost full. Clearly, business had not been good. Her sad, drawn expression told the whole story. But, at the sight of the visitors, the Christmas tree, and the presents, her face lit up, first with bewilderment, and then with wonder. On her knees, she touched the presents with trembling fingers, then timidly looked up. Her golden curls framed the ecstatic light in her big blue eyes. She asked, in a shy voice:

'Are these for me?'

'It would seem so, my child,' answered John Hopper with a fatherly smile.

'My Goodness,' she gasped, 'it's not possible. Who could have . . . ?'

'Father Christmas, of course!' sniffed Tommy, shrugging his shoulders.

"Slowly, Sidonie raised her head to look at the rich merchant. After a moment of hesitation, she asked:

'It was you, Mr. Sterling, wasn't it?' . . .

"Then she fell down at his feet. Her beautiful blond hair spread over the merchant's polished shoes as she sobbed:

'Thank you, Mr. Sterling, thank you a thousand times . . . You are too good to us. . . . '

"Trembling with rage, the old merchant mumbled something incoherent, then turned on his heels and stormed out of the room.

"Outside, he sought in vain for any signs of trickery. He asked his companions to examine everything: the windows, the tracks in the snow, the warehouse wall, the banks of the river. All their efforts were in vain. Not a single clue was to be found. As for the ruts and the prints, they appeared to have been left by a sleigh drawn by horses or reindeer. Everyone was agreed on that point, even though the tracks had been somewhat smoothed over by the most recent fall of snow. The problem was: how had they appeared on a long stretch of virgin snow, four yards wide, and in such a short space of time?

"The absence of tracks on the edge of the bank, and the fact that the river was nearly two feet below, ruled out the possibility of arriving by way of the river, or any other manoeuvre that involved landing—such as some complicated scheme for making tracks by digging holes with a stick. What's more, the presence of a visitor in the Buckley house had been proved, not to mention the gradual appearance and disappearance of the ruts. The mystery could not be explained in any rational manner. The little group had indeed witnessed a miracle: the visit of 'Father Christmas'!

"But Sterling still refused to admit it. Once home, he had subjected little Tommy to a serious interrogation. A waste of time. The little boy stuck to his guns and refused to budge: he had indeed seen Father Christmas come down from the sky. Besides, he argued with a child's irrefutable logic, why was Mr. Sterling so surprised? Hadn't he himself announced the arrival of Father Christmas, after he had heard the bells outside? And didn't all the other facts speak for themselves? Disconcerted, and with his nerves on edge, Sterling gave up.

"The next day he admitted having passed a very bad night. Several times he had heard the bells ringing! The next night the same thing happened. But he was not the only one. Everyone in the house had heard them. The sounds appeared to come from inside the house: more precisely, from the direction of the chimney. The following day, things became clearer. That morning, Sterling found, in front of the hearth amongst the ashes and soot, a thick parcel carefully wrapped. Its size was out of all proportion to its contents, which turned out to be minuscule: a one-shilling coin. No-one knew where it had come from. Nevertheless, it seemed obvious that the mysterious sender had come down the chimney. Anyone of normal build could have done it.

"From that moment on, Sterling appeared to be seriously shaken, yet he was no less angry for all that. He searched frantically all over the large house, ears cocked, eyes wary. His heavy steps resonated on the stairs and in the corridors of each floor. He vowed that he would soon track down the intruder and administer a severe punishment.

"Apparently he was successful in making contact, but the meeting did not go as planned. As night was falling that same day, a loud shout disturbed the peaceful calm of the house. In the library, Margaret Hopper was telling the children a story. Her husband John, who was smoking a cigar in the lounge, arrived first on the scene, followed immediately by Ronald Ark, who had been resting in his bedroom. Sterling lay seriously hurt on the edge of the bank in front of the house. At the very moment Hopper appeared on the doorstep, the unfortunate merchant slid down into the icy waters of the river. His corpse was later fished out downstream, and it was discovered that he had suffered bruises to the body and a fractured skull.

"Who had attacked him? For those who witnessed the tragic events, it was a new mystery. Although it was snowing, there were no footprints near the spot where Sterling had been found. Not even his own! The only possible explanation appeared to be that the killer had steered a small boat downstream and deposited Sterling on the bank before dealing him a mortal blow. But that wasn't the question on the minds of the police. By the time they arrived, one hour after the discovery, snow had blanketed the area with a coat too thick for there to be any hope of finding any tracks. Furthermore, the notion that there had been no footprints seemed so bizarre that the investigators did not take it seriously.

"When we told them about the incredible events of Christmas Eve, how a visitor had come down from the sky in a sleigh drawn by reindeer, they took no notice because they were convinced that all the witnesses were victims of hallucinations. Nevertheless, they continued their investigations. They first suspected Buckley, on the assumption that he had sought revenge against his old employer. But Sterling's ex-employee had a cast-iron alibi. At the time of the murder he had been in his usual pub with his regular drinking companions, and in no state to have committed any crime.

"The police had to look elsewhere. Ronald Ark, the importer, had no motive whatsoever. With the brutal death of his friend, he lost one of his best customers. In contrast, Margaret, her brother's sole heiress, now found herself in possession of a considerable fortune. Luckily for her, she could not have been the assailant herself, because Tommy and Theodore had been with her at the time of the crime. But her husband could have done the deadly deed. No charges, however, could be brought against him. The placid John Hopper and his wife would soon be able to enjoy Drake Sterling's wealth in peace and quiet. The couple made a charitable gesture by putting Buckley in charge of the fabric shop. The ex-salesman recovered his dignity and gave up alcohol for good. The story, as you can see, ended well for everyone except, of course, Sterling! The years have passed and, little by little, this incredible unsolved mystery has been forgotten."

Behaegel's account was followed by a lengthy silence, but the phrase 'incredible unsolved mystery' echoed in our bewildered thoughts. The story was, as he said, more like a fairy tale than a real-life crime. Owen had already confronted many strange cases but never, as far as I can recall, one that involved a 'miracle'. But the events, as described, did indeed appear miraculous!

I gave Behaegel my impression, which was of total bewilderment in the face of such an extraordinary story, fully expecting a similar reaction from my friend. But Owen did not appear disturbed by the bizarre events. On the contrary, Benhaegel's story seemed to have reinvigorated him. Cheeks flushed, he played distractedly with the statuette of a Greek god on the mantelpiece.

"Your account is admirable in many respects," he said suddenly. "For the average mortal, it defies logic and is a remarkable challenge to the mind." He turned to me with a patronising smile. "Isn't that so, Achilles? You seem utterly baffled by this mystery."

"Are you claiming to have solved it?" I replied tersely.

Ignoring my question, he turned to Behaeghel:

"And you say nobody has ever found the key to the puzzle?"

"No," said our guest, shaking his head. "But it hasn't been for want of trying. Several amateur detectives, having learned of the affair, tried to solve it, but without success."

"So *nobody*, today, knows the answer?" insisted Owen.

A half-smile on his lips, Behaegel's eyes narrowed:

"One would think you knew something, Burns."

"Of course," confirmed my friend with great assurance. "I know that the events go back thirty years, and that you have changed the names of some of the players, because you were personally involved. In other words, you were one of the witnesses quoted in the story."

"Little Tommy!" I exclaimed.

"Little Tommy or Theodore," corrected Owen. "In view of your age, you must be one of the two!"

"Yes," admitted Behaegel. "You've spotted it. Frankly, I was expecting that you would. However," he continued defiantly, "that still doesn't explain the riddle of 'Father Christmas' and the mysterious flying sleigh."

"I know everything," repeated Owen, mischievously. "Sincerely, Behaeghel, I'm pleased to have made your acquaintance, and that of your charming spouse and accomplice, the fair Lydia . . . when you see her next in Paris, don't forget to give her my regards. Please tell her also that, as an artist, I very much admire flower girls."

Taken aback, Behaegel sat with his mouth open for several moments, then stammered:

"So, you really do understand?"

With a self-deprecating shrug, Owen replied:

"But of course, my dear fellow. Like me, you are an artist, and artists understand one another! The tall, dreamy Theodore was you, of course! I was like that myself at that age, shy and somehow different from the others. I couldn't help but recognise you! You and your accomplice Lydia whom you have named Sidonie in your account. The similarity of two female names, one from the country of Croesus and the other from ancient Sidon, could not have escaped the notice of a classic scholar such as myself! And, what's more, you recounted the facts with enough honesty that I was quickly on the scent. You made a point of honour to cover all the facts and psychological details necessary to solve the puzzle. For the grudge you held against your uncle was not just about his greed and his contemptible behaviour towards his fellow creatures, but most of all about his attitude towards Father Christmas! Not only did he not believe in him, but *it was he that had told you he didn't exist!* In just a few words, he had shattered your little universe! And you could never forgive him for that!"

There was a nostalgic gleam in Behaegel's eye.

"When I was eleven, I still believed in Father Christmas. I believed in the stars and in silver sleighs making tracks in the sky. When he told me the truth I was devastated. The fairy tales of my infancy had just come to an end. I had gone through the mirror in the opposite direction, into the sinister grey world of adults."

"I'm sure your vocation as playwright had its origins there!" exclaimed Owen, laughing. "You should be grateful to your uncle!"

"Yes, in some ways. His coldness must have helped forge my character."

"And your wife, too. It was because of him that you met, wasn't it?"

Behaegel had a faraway look in his eye as he answered:

"When I first saw her, she seemed to have stepped right out of a fairy tale. She was like—"

"Like the flower girl we saw not long ago," said Owen, turning towards the window. "Nobody understands your state of mind better than I, my friend, believe me. As soon as you met her, you felt instinctively she would become your accomplice for life, and the two of you quickly combined your artistic talents to play a dirty trick on Sterling. It's obvious what was motivating little Lydia. Your uncle's attitude towards her must have revolted you, but most of all you bore a grudge because he had shattered your illusions. It must have seemed like poetic justice to prove to him that Father Christmas did exist, and to bring home to him the cruelty of his behaviour towards Lydia's father. You worked out the details of your plan as soon as you arrived in your uncle's house with your parents, in other words at the beginning of the week: the day before the fire in the laundry. Which was not, by the way, an unimportant event. Seasoned observers such as myself know that, in such cases, it is the consequences that are important, namely the disappearance of clothes and *sheets*—which are, incidentally, the classic props for playing at ghosts.

"Obviously, if you had simply taken the sheets without the cover of the fire, their disappearance would have caused suspicion. Be that as it may, I will explain what you did. Since the beginning of the week, it had been snowing in London. Frequent falls of snow, interspersed with morning freezes, had the effect of forming a thin surface crust. On the afternoon of Christmas Eve, you arranged for a delivery man to deposit inside the Buckley residence the parcels that were discovered there later that evening. I assume that he came by sleigh, pulled by donkeys or horses. Without doubt, it was purely the witnesses' imagination which caused them to speak of *reindeer*, because those large ruminants are, to my knowledge, extremely rare in London!

"Once the tracks had been made in the snow, you and your accomplice arrived by boat armed with five or six sheets, probably stitched together two-by-two in order to get the right dimensions. By unrolling them slowly and carefully, you were able to cover the entire width of the path –whose surface had been somewhat hardened by the cold, remember—over a distance of ten yards or so. The operation took place in two or three steps. It was first necessary to cover the central section of the tracks before the next snowfall, in order to preserve the clear tracks at their original depth; then, a little later, the end sections were covered so that the tracks, slightly filled by the snow, appeared less deep.

"After those preliminary arrangements, it was Lydia—otherwise known as Sidonie—who acted alone, because you were with your family in your uncle's house. Shortly before midnight, the host and his guests went out onto the doorstep to get some fresh air, and observed that there were no marks of any kind on the surrounding snow. At this point, the sheets were completely invisible under the snow. Once the little group had gone back inside, Lydia—still in the boat— tugged gently on the sheets, unveiling the tracks that had been made that afternoon on the surface of the path; the tracks at each end being shallower because the sheets were laid later, as I have said. It was still snowing a little, which would help eliminate any traces of the trickery. Now all she had to do was to ring some sleigh bells and disappear from sight for a while. The subsequent reactions of little Tommy and his conversation with Sterling seemed natural enough in view of the circumstances, but I'll wager that you did influence the lad to behave as he did. Your close relationship, despite the five years' difference in age, must have helped. And later on, when you were pointing out the 'miraculous' nature of the tracks and Sidonie's presents, a few judicious remarks such as 'you see, Father Christmas exists' succeeded in convincing Tommy that he had indeed seen him, to the point that he continued to insist that was the case when Sterling questioned him afterwards. The act that 'Sidonie' put on when she came home and feigned surprise at all those presents at the foot of the tree, and her gratitude to Sterling for 'his' generosity, undoubtedly foreshadowed the superb artist she later became. Truly, Behaegel, you are a very lucky man."

The playwright, embarrassed yet flattered, acknowledged the compliment. Owen, who had reached the window, looked sadly down on the snow-covered street below.

"Who knows," he murmured, "maybe one day I will have a chance like that, meeting someone with whom I can share *a discreet but profound complicity.*"

There was a long silence in the room, an almost conspiratorial silence between my two companions who appeared to understand each other perfectly. I cleared my throat noisily before I spoke:

"At the risk of appearing stupid, Owen, I would like you to clear up a few details. For example, the fire that broke out all by itself in the Buckleys' hearth. Despite all your explanations, I haven't managed to understand how that was done, given that all the doors and windows were shut on the inside."

My friend shrugged his shoulders:

"That's a minor detail, which could be explained any number of ways. But I assume it was done in the simplest way imaginable, by preparing a stack of dry wood and paper in the fireplace, so that Lydia, at the right moment could climb up onto the roof and throw a lighted taper down the chimney."

Owen turned to Behaegel, who nodded in agreement:

"She has always been as agile as a cat."

The silent understanding and acquiescence between my two companions, who scarcely knew each other, was starting to get under my skin. Scarcely containing myself, I asked through clenched teeth:

"There's also the 'minor detail' of old Sterling's murder! Not only do I fail to understand how it was done, but I must also point out that talk of murder means talk of a murderer! And, if I've grasped what you've been saying, the culprits are none other than . . . ."

While I was speaking, I was glaring in the direction of Behaegel. Owen chuckled, and exclaimed:

"It does seem entirely possible, Achilles, that you haven't understood after all! As I told you, the sole intention of this children's prank was to make Sterling believe in Father Christmas. After the success of the sleigh in the sky, having seen how much the merchant had been shaken, our little tricksters decided to keep going. So 'Theodore' discreetly arranged for a sleigh bell to ring frequently in the chimney. It worked so well that the victim ended up believing in that same Father Christmas! The symbolic coin wrapped in that thick gift-parcel was the final straw. The merchant went to find where it came from, there, where Father Christmas traditionally lands: on the roof, by the chimney.

"Trembling with rage and, doubtless, also with cold, Sterling inevitably lost his footing. He slid the length of the sloping the roof, like a child on a toboggan, and plunged to the ground not far from the doorstep, near the river bank. His last throes before falling into the river; the heartrending scream as he fell; the bruises and the fractured skull; all these were misinterpreted by witnesses who were at their wits' end following the events of Christmas Eve. But there was no excuse for the Scotland Yard investigators.

If one of them had believed just a little in Father Christmas, he would have raised his eyes heavenwards for proof of his visit! And he would have seen suspicious tracks on the edge of the roof!"

Owen shook his head despondently, and added in a weary voice:

"People will never understand that life itself is a fairy tale . . . "

RIPPERMANIA

" . . . And now I'm having the nightmares more and more frequently. Twice in one night, even. I wake up panting and perspiring, and it takes me several minutes to get back to normal. In my head, there's always this infernal merry-go-round. Women with raucous laughter are making fun of me. They're heavily made up, they wear outlandish hats, their clothes are gaudy . . . ."

Alain Parmentier went quiet for an instant. Stretched out almost motionless on the couch, he had been talking without a break for almost an hour. The man sitting next to him on the chair with the armrests had said not a word, contenting himself with the occasional nod, which might have been approving or merely thoughtful. Of average weight, and in his forties, he was at least ten years older than Alain Parmentier, but with considerably less hair. His clear blue eyes which betrayed no sentiment behind the silver-rimmed spectacles, his discreet and elegant appearance, his careful gestures, his courtesy bordering on indifference, all conspired to create an impression of impersonality. Everything about him and around him was neutral, completely neutral. Thus, he corresponded exactly to the image his patients had of him as they pressed the buzzer at the entrance, where they could read: Charles Linck, psychiatrist.

For Alain Parmentier, it was the third time he had pressed the buzzer in less than two weeks. Their first meeting, so to speak, had lasted two hours, during which time Dr. Linck had observed a total silence except at the very end, when he had told his new patient with a thoughtful, very professional air:

"It's too soon to make any diagnosis. Come again next week. Same day, same time? Thank you. That will be fifteen hundred francs."

Don't they say silence is golden? And speech is silver? During the second session, Dr. Linck interrupted his patient's monologue with a 'You shouldn't have done, but pray continue' which cost just as much as the silence of the previous week.

"Some grey areas are starting to become clearer," Dr. Linck had said in a very solemn manner as he was showing his patient out. "But I prefer to reserve my opinion for the moment. Can you come back in a week's time?"

"That's too long, doctor, I'm at the end of my tether. Couldn't I come back tomorrow?"

"Tomorrow? Alas! That's not possible, although—"

"Doctor, I need you, you have to listen to me. It does me good, it calms me down."

"Very well. Come round this evening."

Alain Parmentier stopped a moment to stare into Dr. Linck's spectacles, which were reflecting the light from the lamp, and replied:

"I'm not always in my bed when I wake from these bad dreams: sometimes I'm following the walls of some small street in the area! And I'm fully dressed! Raincoat and hat! I'm as exhausted, reeling, heart beating wildly as if I'd just run five miles! And I don't know what I've done or how I got there. Doctor, can't you understand how serious it is? What can it all mean? And also, I have the impression that I've done something awful . . . something truly awful."

Dr. Linck stroked his chin thoughtfully.

"Tell me again about your dreams."

"Well, I'm wandering the streets, dark streets, not like those here. Much narrower, more higgledy-piggledy, badly paved. With carriage entrances, dead-ends, hidden courtyards, all very badly lit. It's often foggy . . . . "

"Don't you sometimes hear horses' hooves?"

"Now that you say it, yes, I think I do."

"A horse in harness, a hackney cab?"

"Yes . . . yes, that's it, a hackney cab. There are no cars, just horse-drawn cabs, you're right. Actually they're quite rare, because everything happens at dead of night. The streets are deserted, there's not a living soul, except sometimes a tramp or a strumpet."

"And these strumpets as you call them, don't they wear plumed hats?"

"Yes, I think so. I walk, I'm alone, I'm afraid but . . . how can I put this? I seem to derive satisfaction from this state of panic. The area is ill-frequented, dangerous even, yet . . . yet this fear, this disquiet, brings me a certain pleasure. At each intersection, in each alley, I imagine there to be someone lurking in the darkness, waiting for the right moment to commit the worst crimes, the worst atrocities and . . . and . . . . "

"I see," Dr. Linck nodded with a smile. "I must confess it's rather rare for me get to the root of the problem so quickly. But everything points to my diagnosis being correct. Nevertheless, we need to do one last test. I suggest, while you're waiting, we take a short break so that you'll be completely relaxed. Take a seat, smoke a cigarette, thumb through a magazine, I'll be with you in a moment."

The psychologist got up, walked across the room, and disappeared behind a door leading to his private flat.

Alain Parmentier sat up and followed the doctor's advice. After a few puffs on his cigarette, he picked up the newspaper—dated the day before—and started to turn the pages aimlessly. One article, however, grabbed his attention.

After his seventh attack, the ripper is still at liberty
Even if the police are still guessing as to the identity of the monster who has been roaming the seediest parts of the port for several months now, they are in no doubt as to the motive. The fact that the seventh victim is yet again a prostitute cannot be purely a matter of chance. The inspector in charge of the investigation confirms that they are dealing with one of those sexual maniacs so prevalent in the history of crime. A theory borne out by the very nature of his acts. The latest victim was found with her throat slit from ear to ear, and her body covered with wounds, the nature of which decency prevents us from describing in greater detail. We sympathise with those of our fellow citizens obliged by their very profession to walk the streets at night . . . .

A gentle tinkle coming from the telephone on the small table attracted Alain Parmentier's attention. The instrument must have been connected to a line in Dr. Linck's flat, and apparently the good doctor had just hung up at the end of a short conversation. After a few seconds of reflection, Parmentier put down the newspaper, went over to the coat-rack, picked up his hat, examined the inside, replaced it, and went back to lie on the couch, at which point Dr. Linck came back into the room.

"Right. Now we're ready to start," he said, with a beaming smile. "The principle of the test is very simple. I read out a word and you say another immediately, without thinking. The spontaneity of your responses is the key to success."

"A sort of association of ideas?"

"That's exactly what it is," agreed Dr. Linck, sitting down in his chair. "Are you ready? Perfect. I'll start: *woman* . . . . "

"Strumpet"

"*Fog.*"

"Murder."

"*Light.*"

"Gaslamp."

"*Doctor.*"

"Scalpel."

"*Footstep.*"

"Murderer."

"*Cobblestone.*"

"Blood."

"*Wound.*"

"Throat."

"*Knife.*"

"Stomach."

"*London.*"

"Whitechapel."

The doctor raised his hand to stop:

"No need to go any further. There's no longer any shadow of a doubt: you're afflicted with rippermania."

"Rippermania?" echoed Alain Parmentier, his eyes wide. "What's that?" Dr. Linck smiled indulgently.

"It's the sickness, for want of a better word, of ripperologues. And a ripperologue is someone who is intensely interested in the case of Jack the Ripper. Does that name mean anything to you?"

"Of course, but . . . . "

"Let me guess. All you know about this sinister individual is that he slaughtered prostitutes with an indescribable violence and his identity was never discovered, am I right?"

"Well, yes."

"That's all most people know about the subject. But the mere name often evokes, subconsciously, a whole universe. The London of the last century, with its hackney cabs, its fog, its taverns, its dark side streets . . . and then this crazed killer, who committed the most hideous atrocities and whose motive and identity remain a complete mystery. That's a horribly fascinating mix, don't you agree? Because you are fascinated, lured by the person and the times, there's no longer the slightest doubt. Rest assured, you're not the only one: ripperologues are far more numerous than you might think. The majority of them are historians or retired policemen, who continue indefatigably to turn over every detail of this puzzling affair in order to solve the mystery. They claim it's purely for historic purposes, but I suspect other, more subtle, motives for their search. Generally, they meet in London every year and make a pilgrimage to the different murder sites: Buck's Row, 29 Hanbury Street, Berner Street, the corner of Mitre Square, Miller's Court."

Dr. Linck stopped, and a curious silence reigned. Alain Parmentier broke it suddenly, a distant look in his eyes:

"Tell me about this business again, doctor."

Dr. Linck obliged, going into a monologue that lasted almost an hour, with his patient hanging on every word.

"So what must I do now, doctor?" said Parmentier when the doctor had finished. "What remedy do you prescribe?"

"To start with, you should get hold of all the books on the subject, so that you know all there is to know about it. Then, as soon as possible, take two weeks off and spend them in London. Two weeks is the minimum. Try and absorb the atmosphere of Whitechapel. Afterwards, come and see me again. Between now and then, I believe things will get better, much better."

"Thank you, doctor. Thank you for everything," said Alain Parmentier as he took his leave. "I feel better already, now that I know."

With a curious smile on his face, he stepped quickly into a lift which took him down five floors to the street. Outside, it was already night. Two men in raincoats greeted him as he left the building.

"We were beginning to worry, boss," said the younger of the two. "Another half hour and we would have come up to have a look. So, is it him?"

"String me up and hang me if that's not the monster that's been killing the girls," replied Inspector Alain Parmentier. "He's sick, fascinated by the character of Jack the Ripper. I finally got him to break his silence. He didn't open his mouth during the first two sessions, but then, once he got started on his favourite subject, there was no way to stop him. He recited the whole history of the Ripper with a depth of detail that left no possible doubt."

The inspector removed his hat and took out a miniature tape recorder:

"Our whole conversation is there, there won't be any doubt in your mind once you've heard this! There's enough to convince even the most reluctant of juries!"

"In fact, boss," said the other plain clothes policeman, "you still haven't told us how you got on his trail."

"Sheer luck, I admit. I had seen him a few times at my local bookstore, and he drew my attention because he always ordered books on English criminology. I made discreet enquiries of the store owner, who told me the fellow was a psychologist. That was the trigger. I've always found people like that have a complete blind spot when it comes to their own case. I fooled him and strung him along in a way I couldn't have done with someone with ordinary common sense."

"Meanwhile, he stung you for nearly five thousand francs for just three sessions. Half what I make in a month. I don't know who fooled who!" observed the younger detective.

"And I'm not sure," scoffed his colleague, "that you'll be reimbursed, particularly if he's not our man!"

"I'm telling you," said Parmentier tersely, "that I'm quite sure I'm right. Anyway, enough talk. We'll soon see. Is everyone in place?"

The two detectives nodded.

"And our 'goat'?"

"Sergeant Belmont?" laughed the younger one. "I'm sure she can't wait to meet the 'wolf'!"

"Right. I'll just go and have a word with her. The success of the operation rests on her shoulders."

"Or on her pretty little neck."

"Very funny. Well, I'll see you shortly. Be on the alert. He could be out any moment now."

In a doorway in a nearby side street, under a street-lamp, the inspector found Sergeant Brigitte Belmont. For the occasion, she had forsaken her uniform for an outfit appropriate to the world's oldest profession, which actually suited her quite well, showing off her perfect legs and delectable curves.

"Good," said Parmentier, somewhat hot under the collar. "I see that you've made quite an effort. I've never seen such a pretty little tart. Congratulations, Sergeant!"

"Oh, sir, you do say the nicest things!" replied the blonde beauty, teasingly.

"Please, Brigitte, this is no time for joking. We know what we have to do now. I'm sure I don't have to repeat your instructions, you must know them by heart. You contrive to let him see you and approach you. As soon as he makes any kind of sudden move, even if it seems harmless—for we can't afford the slightest risk—you throw yourself on the ground and shout for help. My men will be there right away and will take care of him. But you mustn't move a muscle, Brigitte, until I arrive, is that understood?"

"Yes, chief. But tell me, are you sure he'll come?"

"I already told you he's a frequent visitor to the local whores, didn't I? So, I'd be amazed if he wasn't attracted to—to what you were chosen for. Right, I have to go, but once again, follow your instructions to the letter!"

Five minutes later, Parmentier and his two colleagues were waiting for their prey at the entrance of the building.

"What makes you think he'll come out tonight, boss?"

"He goes for a walk every other night, and with the conversation we've just had I'd be surprised if he didn't get ants in his pants. Wait, there he is!"

The three detectives followed the psychologist to the top of the narrow side street. And, as expected, they saw him stop in front of the doorway. Less than ten seconds later, a terrifying scream broke the silence. Parmentier blew the whistle which was at his lips, while the two other detectives ran to the spot.

So started a manhunt which did not last long: Dr. Linck, who had run at the sound, lacked the training of the two young policemen, who had been chosen for their athletic qualities. But, while the pack was chasing the fugitive, Inspector Parmentier himself stopped at the doorway where Sergeant Belmont had fallen.

"Well done, my sweet," he said quietly, "I hope you're alright."

"Not even a scratch," said the young blonde, getting up. "And I didn't move a muscle, just like you said. Followed my instructions to the letter."

"Very good. We've got him now. It's a question of minutes. And all thanks to you. You were terrific."

"Oh, you know, I didn't really do anything. I screamed as soon as he moved his hand."

"Perfect."

"But, tell me, don't you think it's a bit of an exaggeration to say we caught him red-handed?"

"His running away is a confession in itself."

"Between you and me, in his place, with all the whistle-blowing and people running towards him, I think I might have run as well."

"In any case, this series of murders had to come to an end, and with an arrest, obviously. It couldn't go on. Everyone was becoming suspect, even the town's most respectable citizens, and even members of the police force."

"But what if we've got the wrong man?" asked Brigitte. "By the way, he didn't strike me—"

"You obviously haven't understood a thing, my sweet," said Inspector Parmentier calmly, taking a bright object out of his pocket.

Five minutes later, he joined his men as they took the suspect away in handcuffs, thrashing about wildly and proclaiming his innocence at the top of his voice.

"My God!" exclaimed the younger detective, seeing his chief returning alone, a grim expression on his face. "Don't tell me that—"

"Yes," said the inspector, through gritted teeth. "Take him away, this bastard, before I skin him alive! This piece of filth, this scum, had just enough time to slit her throat! Her blood was everywhere, the poor girl. Look, I even got some on my hands as I tried to lift her up!"

MURDER IN COGNAC

It was a lovely summer evening in the Charentes, and a Talbot saloon was driving slowly along a quiet country road. The driver, a rather corpulent individual of some fifty years, was scrutinising his surroundings with a look that was at once exasperated and hesitant. His round, ruddy face, dripping with perspiration, testified to the stifling heat inside the car.

Under normal circumstances, Inspector Archibald Hurst of Scotland Yard would have appreciated a break in his hectic routine that allowed him to enjoy green fields and vineyards bathed in quiet sunlight. He would have enjoyed the discreet charm of the many villages with their Roman churches built of white stone and the beautifully sculpted facades. But that was precisely the rub: for more than an hour, he had done nothing but go round in circles through these same villages, trying to find the hamlet where his friend Twist was staying. Dr. Alan Twist, doctor of philosophy, but, above all, amateur detective, whose specialty was helping the police solve particularly baffling crimes.

"Where the devil is he hiding?" hissed the inspector through clenched teeth, the knuckles of his hands white on the steering wheel. Frustrated and disoriented, Hurst was on the point of giving up. That was when, by one of those curious strokes of fate, he suddenly found the aforementioned hamlet before him. Most of the houses, solidly built of rough-cut stone, seemed to belong to an earlier time. The detective smiled as he recognised the classic rural setting so dear to his friend's heart.

A few minutes later, he had joined him, in the welcome cool of a rustic lounge, and was sipping a glass of cognac.

"What incredible luck to find you here!" declared the inspector, now more relaxed. "I knew you were on holiday in France, but I didn't know where! Imagine my surprise this morning when Superintendent Charles told me an eminent London criminologist was staying in one of the old houses around here! I jumped in my car straight away to come and say hello."

A smile crossed the face of his host, a tall thin man in his fifties with an alert look in his eye and a magnificent moustache on his upper lip:

"Eminent London criminologist," he repeated, nodding his head. "Really, my old friend, you have a gift for finding the right phrase, if I may say so—"

"Those were the superintendent's words."

"—because, in fact, I'm trying to be the exact opposite. What I'm really looking for is to be neither criminologist, nor Londoner, nor eminent! Just a bit of peace and quiet, so I can sample the gastronomy of the region and its justly celebrated spirits under the best possible conditions."

"What can I say? It's the price of fame! Your reputation has preceded you, my dear Twist!" He looked around the room. "I must say, it's damned comfortable here! You would never tell from the outside."

"It's very pleasant," agreed Twist. "I'm glad you like it. If you feel like staying, let me know. I'd be delighted to put you up for a few days."

After a quick glance at the ceiling, supported by old oak beams at least a hundred years old, the detective replied:

"It's just a little bit too ancient for my taste."

"There's a telephone," Twist pointed out.

"I know. The superintendent told me. It's possible someone might try to call me while I'm here."

"Oh? You wouldn't be here on official business, by any chance?"

"Yes and no. Like you, I chose to take my holiday in France this year. As I was already here, I went to see my sister-in-law whom I haven't seen since the end of the war. I think I already told you about my brother who was killed at Dunkirk? His young widow left England to come back here to her native Charentes, where she remarried. Her second husband, Charles, was just an ordinary policeman at the time. Since then, he's risen in the ranks. Just recently, he was named superintendent for the Cognac region. But right now he has a rather embarrassing case on his hands, which has put a bit of a damper on things. A rather unusual problem, in fact."

"A problem which has now become your own?"

"Let's just say that I was rash enough to offer him some advice. It's a rather delicate matter. It's about protecting a certain Michel Soudard, a retired wine grower. For a week he's been barricading himself in his house, because he has been receiving threats."

While he was talking, Hurst had been about to reach out for his glass on the table when his host suddenly shouted out:

"Hermes! No!"

Twist's warning was in vain. A shadow came hurtling out of one of the corners of the room and within inches of knocking over the inspector's glass. The disobedient Hermes was in fact a black cat who seemed to have taken an instant liking to the visitor. Purring with delight, he crawled across the inspector's plump thighs and curled up in his lap. But the little cat's feelings were not reciprocated. Eyes popping, Hurst looked as if he had been electrocuted.

"He hasn't got the plague, Archibald! You can stroke him."

The inspector lifted his hand hesitantly and mumbled:

"You know that I can't stand these animals. I can't help it."

"You are as suspicious as the villagers here! When I arrived here, this tomcat was a bag of bones. Nobody wanted anything to do with him because he's black. In other words, the very incarnation of the Devil."

"I thought that black cats were supposed to be lucky?"

"Not here in France: they believe the exact opposite, and that's why this innocent creature was dying of hunger and deprived of affection."

"With you, I'm sure he'll catch up the lost years! But now, Twist, I would be eternally grateful if you would find him a different cushion."

A few moments later, after having installed His Furry Majesty in another room, Twist returned to his friend and observed in a rather caustic voice:

"There, the *Devil* is gone, you can relax now."

Nevertheless, Hurst still seemed perturbed, and his ruddy face remained covered in perspiration despite the comparative coolness of the room.

"I'm not so sure," he replied, cautiously. "I already feel I'm dealing with Lucifer himself."

"You're referring to your 'delicate matter'?"

"Yes."

"Well, if that's your wine grower's enemy, you're right to be worried."

"From what I've heard, the individual who has sworn to eliminate Michel Soudard is as intimidating as Satan himself: Philippe Faux, who some have named the Magician of Crime."

"A dangerous killer?"

"No, but he might be, and that's why we're taking the matter seriously.

The fellow is diabolically clever, a virtuoso prestidigitator whose hobby is criminology. He's read everything to do with crime, true or fictional, and has an extraordinary library on the subject."

Twist leaned back in his armchair and said approvingly:

"Sounds like the epitome of a formidable adversary. But what has he against this Michel Soudard?"

The policeman drained his glass, settled down in his armchair, and commenced:

"Let me begin at the beginning. Michel Soudard is a retired wine grower who had other passions as well as wine in his life. After the sale of his vineyard—which fetched a good price because his brandy had a fine reputation—he has been able to devote himself entirely to his favourite interests, spiritualism and the occult, which he nevertheless pursues in a measured, rational manner. He launched the Association for the Investigation of Paranormal Phenomena, which you may have heard of?"

"Yes. They pursue fraudulent spiritualists and other charlatans, don't they?"

"Precisely. And Philippe Faux passes himself off as some sort of wizard with exceptional powers, capable of prodigious feats. He performs regularly in public, for free, no doubt in order to consolidate his reputation as a philanthropist and savant, thereby luring the gullible, who—alas!—are only too numerous. For we have it on excellent authority that he is very much in demand for private seances. And you may be quite sure he does not perform them purely for love of the art. It's all very healthy for the bank balance, so you can understand why he wasn't exactly thrilled when Soudard interrupted one of his recent sessions. He was in the process of demonstrating his astonishing powers in front of a captivated audience by catching a fish in a transparent bowl of clear water, then changing the water into cognac! For someone like Soudard, a retired Cognac producer, it was like a red rag to a bull. He rushed out from the crowd and pulled a sachet of orange powder from the magician's pocket. Faux reacted furiously. At first he pretended that the sachet was there for another purpose. Then, when Soudard repeated the accusation and made it clear he was going to expose the imposture, he resorted to threats, claiming that it was an outrage and an insult to his mystical powers, and that such an offence warranted the supreme sanction.

The magician thus publicly threatened Soudard, even going so far as to say that he would perish the way he had sinned."

"Meaning cognac?"

"No doubt. Or else fish, because Soudard had also explained the fishing miracle to the audience."

Twist nodded thoughtfully and asked:

"And the police have taken these threats seriously?"

"Yes, because it seems clear that Faux wasn't joking. His reputation and his whole future are at risk."

"If Soudard doesn't die in the next few days, Faux is finished."

"And if something does happen to the old wine grower, it will be my colleague Charles who will be under the gun, because the story about the threat has spread like wildfire throughout Cognac. He would be accused of not having taken the matter seriously. For the time being, he's put the two antagonists under surveillance, just as I advised. One man is watching the Magician of Crime while another is on guard outside the tower where Soudard has barricaded himself in."

"A tower?" asked Twist in astonishment.

"That's right, a tower. In fact, it's the last remnant of a castle built by an eccentric who lived in the region. Our protégé has been living there since he retired, presumably so he could enjoy the peaceful surroundings. In any case, you have to admit that it's an effective refuge. You have to see it to realise how difficult it would be for his enemy to attack him under such circumstances."

"That's what I was thinking, and particularly with a policeman at his heels. Even so, you seem to believe he might succeed in carrying out his threat?"

"Yes," replied Hurst, clenching his fist. "This chap is resourceful. Besides, the precautions taken by Soudard speak for themselves. There would be the devil to pay if our Magician of Crime were able to pull it off."

The telephone rang just at that moment and the inspector froze. Twist crossed the room to pick it up, and turned to his friend:

"It's for you."

Casting a suspicious glance, Hurst hesitated for a second, then grabbed the receiver. He answered with a surly grunt, then stood for several moments in complete silence, a blue vein throbbing in his temple.

"What?" he growled. "How? But it's not possible. For heaven's sake, man, speak more clearly, I can't understand what you're saying."

The conversation continued in the same tone for several seconds more. When Hurst hung up, he looked like a man whom the fates had dealt a terrible blow. He stood stock still, the single wild lock of hair stuck to his forehead.

"Who was it?" asked his host.

"The switchboard operator at the Cognac superintendent's office. The lines there are not very good. But that's not the point. The roof's just fallen in on us."

"Don't tell me that—"

"Yes," cut in Hurst bitterly. "The worst has happened. The Master has won his impossible bet: the old wine grower has just died. It was Soudard himself who broke the news. Before giving up the ghost, he called the superintendent's office and was just able to mumble a few words. Something about a cat and a tin, then nothing. The lads were round there straight away. They found him in his room, lying on the floor, dead. The officer on duty told me they had seen nobody when they approached the tower."

"And how did he die?"

"Poisoned."

Twist removed his pince-nez, and looked enquiringly at his friend:

"While drinking cognac, I presume?"

"Not clear. Because, as I understand it, his last words were 'the cat brought a tin'."

With those words, Inspector Hurst marched resolutely to the door:

"Come on, Twist, there's not a moment to lose. We're going to visit the scene of the crime."

A quarter of an hour later, the inspector's Talbot drew up next to two other cars parked at the base of a tower which was obviously all that remained of a mediaeval castle, solidly built from huge stone blocks, and perched on a rocky outcrop at the edge of a beech wood. The isolation added to the strange allure of the edifice, which looked like nothing less than a windmill without sails. But there was something vaguely menacing about it which evoked its previous use. With respect, no doubt, for its mediaeval origins, it had been fitted with a sharply sloping roof and its thick walls had been pierced by gothic windows; one of these, on the top floor, faced south just above a remarkable wisteria which, clinging to the wall, softened the austere aspect of the tower.

"Soudard's room," explained Hurst, indicating the window with a turn of his head. "There's a small kitchen and bathroom underneath. You can see it there, that small barred window on the east side. There is another identical one on the west side. The front door opens on to the ground floor which is used as a storage area and has just one small barred window. Here we are."

The door in question was ajar and Twist noticed straight away that the wooden frame was broken around the lock. They went in and climbed a dimly-lit spiral staircase to reach the third and highest level, where they found quite a bit of activity taking place. Two uniformed policemen were inspecting a spacious and comfortably furnished room, while a fair-haired young man was leaning over the corpse lying by a washbasin. On seeing the newcomers, he walked over to introduce himself:

"Doctor Vincent Manant. I assume one of you is from Scotland Yard?"

Hurst nodded and briefly introduced himself and his friend.

"The superintendent told me about you," continued Dr. Manant. "He just left for Cognac and asked that you wait for him. The medical examiner should be here soon." A boyish grin spread over his features. "I'm just the village doctor. I happened to run in to Superintendent Charles and he asked me to follow him over here."

Vincent Manant turned towards the body with a sombre expression:

"I knew Michel Soudard personally. I would never have dreamt of finding him under such circumstances."

The victim, a grey-haired man of medium height, was stretched out on the carpet, curled up slightly but with his arms spread out. His silver-rimmed spectacles had fallen from his upturned eyes. Brown traces stained the small washbasin to the left of the body and, to the right, on the floor at the base of a desk, lay an overturned telephone.

"He's been poisoned, I assume?" Hurst asked.

"Yes. Cyanide. No doubt about it, even though, as the superintendent requested, I've only made a superficial examination. Have you noticed that sweet, acrid smell reminiscent of almonds? It's very characteristic."

"And how did it happen?"

The doctor shook his head:

"That's the whole question. As far as I know, the superintendent is very much counting on you to find out. I must admit it all seems very mysterious. At first glance, there doesn't appear to be any cyanide in the room, and it seems pretty clear that nobody could have brought it in without Soudard's knowledge."

The two detectives sized up the room. The practical elements: washbasin, wardrobe, and writing desk, were ranged against the east wall. A bookcase covered the entire west wall. Aside from the books there were various trinkets and strange objects such as a miniature pagoda and an enamelled box containing a cube seemingly suspended in mid air, which Twist's trained eye identified immediately as conjuring accessories. In front of the bookcase was a divan flanked by a standard lamp and a low side-table, on which sat a tray with a glass, a bottle of cognac, and a water carafe which one of the officers was handling with great care. An open book lay face down on the divan. To the south, directly facing the door, was the only window in the room, providing a pleasant view of the Charentes countryside.

"No, the murderer could not have got in here," confirmed the policeman who was examining the tray.

"Was it you who was responsible for guarding the victim?" asked Hurst, with a note of reproach in his voice.

The young officer went pale, but maintained his composure:

"Yes, sir, and I can assure you that no-one came anywhere near the house after the baker left. At that time, Soudard was in perfect health; I saw him collect his baguette from the doorstep at nine o'clock. And after that, up until the superintendent's arrival around four o'clock, I didn't see a living soul. To get into this room, we had to force the front door and this door here, which were both locked on the inside and impossible to open from the outside, as you can see for yourself."

Hurst and Twist both nodded, noting the solid lock on the door. The only sign of the policemen's forced entry was that the screws in the wooden frame had been forced out.

"In short," observed Hurst, "the only way into this room was through the window, which was open, I presume?"

"Yes, just like you would expect in this kind of weather. But I can tell you that nothing human could have come in that way. That's exactly what I kept my eye on the most. And anyway, how could anyone get up there: the room is like a nest twenty-five feet up? By climbing up the wisteria? Not likely. Nobody normal could do it, it's too blooming fragile. Not only that, he couldn't have done it without leaving traces and we didn't find any. It was the first thing we looked for."

"How about with a ladder?"

"No, I would've had to have seen it."

Hurst rubbed the back of his neck:

"So if nobody could have got in, the cyanide must have been in the room already."

"At first sight, there's nothing here that could have been used to store it," added the young policeman almost regretfully, having finished his examination of the tray. "The colourless fluid in that carafe is pure water and what's in the bottom of that bottle is pure cognac. There are a few drops in the glass as well. Obviously, we have to wait for the lab results, but there's no doubt in my mind that they're going to confirm there's no cyanide there. Apart from the bottles and glasses, I don't see how . . . There haven't been any boxes of chocolate or other foodstuffs delivered, and there's an empty tin of sardines in the waste basket. The glass you can see on top of the washbasin is absolutely clean. We still have to examine the floor below carefully, but since the victim was on this floor and cyanide acts very quickly . . . ."

Hurst pulled a face, then questioned the policemen about the phone call the victim had made.

"It was around three o'clock," explained the older officer. "He didn't say much, but we knew straight away that it was serious. A quarter of an hour later, we got here. We broke down the doors and found him just as you see him now. He may have tried to throw up in the sink, but it didn't work out."

"The effect of cyanide is almost immediate," stated Dr. Manant, a finger on his lips. "He must have been already seated on the divan when it happened."

"How do you know that?" asked Hurst, one eyebrow raised questioningly.

"Because of the open book. He felt sick, got up, went to the washbasin, tried to make himself sick, realised the seriousness of the situation, then tried to reach you on the phone."

"What were his last words, exactly?" asked Hurst.

"It was the operator who took the call."

"Yes, I know. He was the one who notified me. But I'm afraid I didn't understand clearly what he was saying."

"Soudard was in very bad shape. He simply said he was about to die."

"What's this over here?" asked Twist, bending down in front of the window. "It looks like a food bowl for some kind of animal. It's empty, but there are a few scraps left."

"Soudard loved cats," replied the doctor. "He told me once that having them around was as good for his health as a glass of the finest cognac. He found their company calming and highly beneficial to his concentration. When I visited him, he would often be deep into a novel, with a cat in his lap."

"Good for him!" commented Twist, picking up the bowl, which he sniffed. He frowned and shook his head. "It smells of sardine, not cyanide."

"Yes, it must be the contents of the tin we found in the wastebasket," suggested the police officer. "We examined it, of course, and it seemed all right."

Twist went to the waste basket, but instead of the sardine tin, he fished out some wrapping paper with labels addressed to the victim. Inspecting it carefully, he asked: "What were Soudard's last words on the telephone?"

"They were very strange," replied the officer, looking down at the bowl. "According to the operator he said literally: 'The cat brought a tin'."

An awkward silence followed, which Hurst eventually broke:

"That's idiotic! It doesn't mean anything! Can you imagine it? A cat proudly bringing a sardine to its master? A sardine doctored with cyanide that Soudard swallowed without thinking, even though he's been a hunted man for the last few days. It doesn't make any sense! And, in any case, the facts prove differently: it was his master that gave the sardine to the cat, not vice versa. Heavens above!"

"Remember, Archibald," interrupted Twist, "the fellow who was threatening him did say he would perish the way he had sinned. Maybe he was referring to fish, because Soudard had exposed that so-called miracle to the audience."

"You're forgetting the cognac!" roared Inspector Hurst, his face flushed. "Look: that tray, with the carafe and the bottle, it might well be that Soudard was trying to reproduce the trick of changing water into cognac, with fatal results.

Twist considered the tray for a moment, then turned to the doctor:

"I take it you knew the victim personally, Dr. Manant?"

The doctor nodded sadly:

"Yes, I would even say we were old friends. We had a common interest."

"What was that?"

"Detective stories. Michel Soudard was almost as avid a collector as I am myself. We actually met in a small second-hand bookshop ten years ago, when I was still a student. It was at about that time that we met Philippe Faux."

"What?" exclaimed Hurst. "Are you telling me that the three of you were friends, and that Soudard got on perfectly well with Faux?"

"Precisely. But that was then. We even collaborated on a book about the crime novel, specifically about impossible crimes and locked rooms. Unfortunately, we then went our separate ways. I went into the medical profession and Michel Soudard decided to specialise in unmasking spiritualist charlatans. And he came up against the most gifted among the three of us."

"Philippe Faux, the Magician of Crime!" declared Hurst in a voice heavy with meaning.

"Quite. In fact, it was Soudard and I who christened him that, because of his inexhaustible knowledge of criminology, and his gift for conjuring. The name stuck, even after he decided to specialise in divining and occult phenomena."

"So, as far as you're concerned, he's a charlatan."

"Without a shadow of doubt. A charlatan who worked out that occultism paid a lot more than crime."

"Are you on speaking terms with him?"

"Officially, yes, if I may put it that way. But in fact we haven't met for quite a while."

The doctor stopped himself for a moment, turned towards the body, and shook his head uncomprehendingly:

"No, really, it's hard to believe. Faux undoubtedly has the talent to commit the perfect crime, but it's one thing to theorise about it and quite another to actually commit one. Especially when you remember how close he and Soudard were in the past. Almost like brothers—"

"Brotherly hatreds are often the worst, that's common knowledge," cut in Hurst. "And besides, Soudard himself took the threats seriously. The evidence shows he was right! Now we need to determine the means: cognac or fish?"

Silence followed Hurst's sententious declaration, but the effect was diminished somewhat by Twist, who started to examine the contents of the bookcase.

"A fine collection," he announced. "There are quite a few rare items here."

His eye fell on the open book lying on the divan. He picked it up, leafed through it, then, addressing Vincent Manant, asked:

"A first edition of Harold Vickers' 'Death Had Wings'. Is it a collector's item?"

"No doubt about it," confirmed the young doctor. "It must be a recent acquisition because I've never seen it in his bookcase. Besides, he would have mentioned it."

"What's strange," observed Twist, picking up the wrapping paper that had been found in the wastebasket, "is that the shape of the book corresponds exactly with the packaging here. According to the postmark, the parcel was sent the day before yesterday, so Soudard presumably got it yesterday—"

"—and it contained this copy of 'Death Had Wings'," finished Manant thoughtfully.

"So, who sent it?" asked Hurst tersely.

"There's no sender's name," replied Twist, examining the wrapping paper. "Nor any note in the book. But, in view of the book's value—at least in the victim's eyes—it must have been a close friend, because booksellers almost always put their name on a parcel."

Superintendent Charles from the Cognac headquarters arrived on the scene, accompanied by the medical examiner. Charles, a small, energetic fifty-year old, who sported a moustache on a face smothered in freckles, seemed immensely relieved at the sight of the London detectives:

"Archibald Hurst and his friend, the eminent criminologist Dr. Twist!" he exclaimed. "Thank God you came! What a strange business, my friends. There's no way to make head nor tail of it! But let's not lose any time: what are your first impressions? Have you solved it already? Frankly, I haven't a clue how the killer pulled it off, although I expect it must have been terribly clever! By the way, I've just seen our prime suspect, and he seems to have a cast-iron alibi!"

Later that afternoon, Philippe Faux welcomed the two detectives to his Cognac apartment which overlooked the Francois I park. The drawing-room where he received them was remarkable for its studied simplicity. Apart from two or three religious objects and Polynesian statues, the place exuded the same peaceful and open serenity as the owner of the property himself. From deep in his armchair, he smiled affably at his guests. With his careful grooming and measured gestures, he could easily have passed for a pastor or a psychiatrist. But a closer inspection would reveal the irony in the magnetic regard of his blue eyes, which contrasted with his rather dark complexion.

However, when the detectives brought up the subject of the murder, he appeared more reflective:

"Yes, it's incredible. I'm still in shock over the news. I couldn't believe my ears when the superintendent came to tell me. As it's turned out, his death was seemingly inevitable."

"Nevertheless, it was you who threatened him, wasn't it, Monsieur Faux?" cut in Hurst.

"Yes, of course. But believe me, gentlemen, at the time I had no idea my powers would be so terribly effective. I could never have imagined that the finger of fate would strike so cruelly at any individual who crossed my path."

"What we believe, Monsieur 'Magician of Crime', is that you knowingly carried out this murder by means of a cunning scheme which we will eventually discover."

"'Magician of Crime'?" repeated Philippe Faux, apparently offended. "It's idiotic to call me that."

"It's the name you're stuck with and which, by the way, seems to fit you like a glove."

A crafty smile appeared on Faux's face:

"Be that as it may, there seems to be no doubt that I was in no position to commit the murder. Thanks to the constant surveillance of the police, the superintendent himself can testify that I haven't left my flat all day."

"What that proves at most is that you didn't get into Soudard's place today. What's more, it seems fair to say that no other human being could have done it either."

"If that's the case, why the devil do you persist in believing that a human being did it?"

Hurst ignored the remark:

"You could very well have set your trap the night, or even days, before. We don't know at this precise moment the method you used but, believe me, we'll find it. I'll put it to you another way, Monsieur Faux, suppose you were innocent . . . "

The magician shrugged his shoulders:

"No problem there, Inspector."

"In your opinion, given the circumstances of the death, could someone have poisoned Soudard by some ingenious method without being present in person at the moment of death?"

"Yes, of course it's possible. But first of all you have to find this famous method!"

"Given that you yourself are a very clever illusionist, you must have some idea."

"It's you who are very clever, Inspector. I might almost believe that I'm not a suspect after all!"

"You're not answering my question. If you can change water into cognac so easily, you should be able to explain how you could change it into a deadly yet seemingly innocuous drink."

"Good God! Such a sacrilegious idea had never occurred to me!"

"And, by the way, you're doubly qualified because you're also considered to be one of the leading experts on crime fiction!"

Their host's features clouded in apparent exasperation:

"Yes, that's true. I did acquire a certain knowledge in that field over the years. At one time, I had read just about everything that had been written on the subject."

"So the *theory* of crime suddenly ceased to interest you?"

"Let's just say that I followed a more lucrative path."

"Do you acknowledge living off the credulity of your clients?"

"What I acknowledge above all, Inspector, is not having the power to kill by means of thought. For if that were the case, believe me, there would be a number of casualties."

Hurst's eyes narrowed:

"Is that a threat?"

There was a cruel gleam in Philippe Faux's eye which vanished as he quickly regained his self-control, and favoured them once again with his affable smile:

"No, Inspector, just an alert. It's not a good thing to try to blacken my name by accusing me of a murder I didn't commit. And now, if there are no more questions, I must ask you to leave. The loss of someone who was once one of my dearest friends has been very painful, whatever you may choose to think."

That evening, the two detectives dined at an inn in the village where Dr. Manant lived, less than a mile from the tower. Superintendent Charles, who had arranged to meet them, had not yet arrived, but they were joined by the doctor instead. There was a pleasant atmosphere in the rustic room where the noise of drinking and carousing mingled with loud commentary about a hotly contested game of *boules*. Inspector Hurst's deep and normally penetrating voice could scarcely be heard:

"What a nerve!" he exclaimed several times. "Trying to make a monkey out of me and threatening me, while all the time he's the main suspect!"

"Philippe Faux has a strong personality," commented Vincent Manant thoughtfully. "You'll have a job catching him off balance; he's very sure of himself."

Hurst shot a wrathful glance at his friend:

"And you, Twist, aren't you going to say anything? I thought you were curiously restrained back there with our suspect."

The criminologist's attention had been caught by the spectacular *tourte flambée au cognac* which the innkeeper had brought over. He nodded appreciatively and took a large bite before answering:

"There wasn't much to be said. Our visit wasn't official, and Faux knew that perfectly well. I thought he actually co-operated to some degree, given that he was being questioned by two complete strangers. That said, I tend to agree with you, Doctor. If he is indeed our adversary, it's not going to be easy to catch him off guard."

"Even if we work out how it was done," added the doctor, hesitantly.

Hurst frowned:

"What's this? Have you an idea?"

"Well, as I said, I do read a lot of detective novels."

Manant was interrupted by the arrival of Superintendent Charles who, exuding confidence, greeted the three of them cheerfully. Hurst's mournful demeanour brought him quickly down to earth

"From the look of it, you've drawn a blank," he said, frowning.

"It's too bad he has such a strong alibi!" grumbled Hurst. "And the worst of it is . . . it's thanks to us! By sticking an officer on his tail, we eliminated him officially from the list of suspects! But tell me, Charles, are you absolutely sure about your man's testimony? Are you sure Faux didn't leave his flat the whole day?"

"Absolutely. Just as I am sure that nobody went in to the tower all day." The superintendent passed his hand nervously through his shock of red hair. "Also, we've examined everything exhaustively: locks, windows, walls, wisteria . . . and not a trace of anything out of the ordinary. We can take it for granted that that the killer used trickery to poison his victim. The question is how he did it, because we haven't found the slightest trace of poison anywhere so far. I'm waiting for the latest test results. Speaking of which, the medical examiner has confirmed it was cyanide, but in a very small quantity or else diluted, because otherwise—given the swift effects of this poison- Michel Soudard would have had great difficulty getting to the phone."

"I think Manant has an idea," interrupted Twist, turning to the doctor, who blushed.

"Yes, but it's only an idea," he stammered in embarrassment. "I wouldn't dream of telling you how to run your enquiry."

Hurst shrugged his shoulders:

"At the point that we're at now . . . Go ahead, Manant."

"It's about that book. Professor Twist deduced correctly that it must have been sent to the victim the day before, and that it must have been done by a close friend. My theory is that whoever sent it didn't wish the victim well."

"I see," said Hurst, eyeing Manant patronisingly. "So the killer used the book to poison Soudard. How the devil did he do it? By sprinkling it with cyanide, so that he inhaled the stuff when he turned the pages? Doesn't sound very likely."

"No, he only had to put the poison around the edges. Certain people, particularly those with dry skin, are in the habit of licking their fingers when they turn the pages. Do you understand? That way, the poison works in small doses. Now, everyone who knew Soudard, myself included, was aware that he had that peculiar habit. Every time I saw him with a book in his hand, he could not stop wetting the tips of his fingers with his lips."

Hurst sat in stunned silence for a second, then his ruddy face lit up:

"Dr. Manant, that's brilliant! Good grief, I think you've found the answer! Thanks to you—"

"No, please, I don't deserve any credit, I just read about it. It was in a detective novel set in a mediaeval monastery, with monks that were more frightening than any of the demons."

"No matter!" declared Hurst with smug satisfaction. "The more I think about it, the more I like the idea! Especially because Faux, who's an avid reader himself, must have got his inspiration from the same book." He turned to his colleagues. "Well, gentlemen, what do you think?"

Charles, looking solemn, agreed:

"Yes, I think we're on the right track. I'll get the lab to look at it right away. What makes it even more likely is that Soudard's sense of smell probably wasn't all that good the last few days. The medical examiner told me he had a bad cold. There were three handkerchiefs found in his pockets. Faux led us on a wild goose chase with all that stuff about perishing the way he had sinned. But in fact, if you use his own words against him he was right: this crime led to his downfall!"

Hurst had wholeheartedly shared Charles' optimism that evening. He was counting the days to the arrest of the culprit, describing his method of attack to his friend, and anticipating how the charlatan who had threatened the police—no matter how subtly—would be brought down a peg or two. When his friend reminded him not to count his chickens before they were hatched, to use the vernacular, he reacted angrily, accusing the other of seeking to undermine his confidence, and the investigation into the bargain. When he deposited Twist at his holiday residence, Hurst was not in a good mood:

"Chicken, cat, fish . . . where would we be if we listened to you? In a menagerie, probably! I'm a police officer, not a zoologist, so you know what you can do with your animals!"

Twist said nothing. His friend had stopped in front of the house. He opened the car door and immediately noticed two green points of light on the doorstep. A mewing broke the silence of the night, and he spoke tenderly:

"Poor Hermes, I've left you by yourself the whole day. You must hate me!"

A low-pitched growl echoed inside the Talbot. Hurst was having great difficulty controlling himself:

"Now you have all the time in the world to share your wild theories with the cat!"

Twist got out of the car. Already regretting his hasty words, the inspector waited for a departing gesture from his companion, but it was not forthcoming. After a few moments, Hurst stole a glance out of the window and was surprised to see his friend standing stock still in the darkness as if he had been changed to stone.

"Something wrong, Twist?" said Hurst. "I hope I didn't upset you with my remarks. We've both had a rough day, and with this heat . . . . "

"You don't realise, Archibald, that your bad moods are often beneficial, one might even say necessary, to stimulate my thoughts."

"If you're referring to the investigation," sneered the policeman, "don't bother. We already know the solution."

"And what if it turns out to be wrong? Anyway, Archibald, I bid you good night. I have a feeling you're going to need to be fresh tomorrow, in view of what's in store."

Archibald Hurst scarcely slept that night. On the few occasions that he dropped off, he was troubled by bizarre dreams about chicken and cats fetching sardines. On awakening, he phoned the superintendent's office and asked for Charles, but the operator told him he had already left. The inspector decided to try and join up with Twist. He had no luck at the house, finding the door closed. It was nearly eleven o'clock by the time he got back to Cognac. The sun was already high in the sky and in the Talbot Hurst started to perspire. He wondered feverishly where the investigation stood and what his colleagues were plotting. Were they going to arrest Faux without him? A wave of anger swept over him at the idea. Having personally arranged for the surveillance of Soudard, with its tragic outcome, it would have been both logical and legitimate to include him. He lunched in a restaurant in the old town near the ancient chateau of the Valois, with his bad mood as his only companion. Then, on returning to the hotel, he practically tore the telegram out of the hands of the receptionist:

Be at the tower at 3 o'clock STOP Arrest of guilty party imminent STOP Charles

Why was it necessary to return to the scene of the crime to arrest the culprit? Why wait for this afternoon? What had his two friends been up to all morning?

Archibald Hurst was still asking himself these questions when he arrived at the tower. "This whole thing stinks of a set up," he growled to himself. Was he about to be present at one of those theatrical arrests so beloved of Twist?

He spotted his friend at the window of the crime room, smiling at him in a manner as strange and sinister as the tower itself, with its grey, forbidding profile rising out of the peaceful Charentes countryside. The surrounding vegetation had yellowed somewhat, as a result of the recent intensely hot days, to the point where even the valiant wisteria mounting assault on the southern flank of the tower appeared to be languishing under the sun's rays. But the building itself, sombre and massive, seemed immune to the sunlight. Would it continue to guard its secrets?

With this thought, Hurst shrugged his shoulders, reminding himself that the mystery had apparently been solved. He walked round the tower to the single entrance, guarded by a uniformed policeman. Another officer saluted him at the top of the stairs, in front of the crime room, where Twist and Superintendent Charles were waiting for him.

"Well, there you are," exclaimed Charles, who seemed even more on edge than before. "We were wondering if you had got our message."

"Yes, just now," grumbled Hurst, frowning. "But what's this all about?"

Charles turned to Twist, who seemed lost in contemplation of the countryside.

"I trust your friend. He's the one directing operations. We're expecting Dr. Manant, Philippe Faux, and—most importantly—the culprit, to join us at any moment."

"What?" exclaimed Hurst, his eyes bulging. "You mean it isn't our famous Magician of Crime?"

There was a sudden silence. Charles seemed on the point of talking, but turned round at the sound of an approaching car's engine. A few moments later, Vincent Manant joined them, cheeks flushed and somewhat out of breath. He greeted the small group, offering his apologies:

"I was detained by a patient. I hope I'm not late?"

"No, not at all, we're still waiting for Philippe Faux," replied Charles curtly.

The young doctor appeared as bemused as Hurst, but the superintendent continued:

"By the way, your idea of a poisoned book was quite clever, but—alas!— wrong. The reports are quite clear. It's reasonably certain that the victim had touched an object or food containing cyanide, because there were slight but distinct traces of the poison on his hands. Unfortunately, there was practically nothing on the book, so it wasn't the poisoned gift we had assumed. But hang on, I hear another car. It must be Faux."

The Magician of Crime arrived. He was undoubtedly an imposing figure. Everything about him was carefully groomed, not a hair out of place. He favoured every member of the small group with his placid and slightly condescending smile, but stopped to linger on Inspector Hurst, who was struggling to appear courteous and relaxed.

For Faux's benefit, Charles went over the red herring concerning the book, to which the magician replied:

"Yes, it's quite clever, even though a little too much in the classic style for me. To be perfectly frank, that explanation would have left me less than satisfied. After all yesterday's commotion, I was expecting rather more."

"Well, I hope you won't be disappointed," said Twist, "because we are expecting the culprit to appear at any moment."

"The culprit?" echoed Faux, in astonishment. "The culprit is going to come here?"

"Let's call him the agent of the crime. I can't unfortunately guarantee his arrival time, but I know he has to eat. Now, since it was about this time yesterday that Soudard departed this life . . . . "

"You love to create a climate of mystery, don't you, Doctor Twist?" asked Faux with one of his unctuous smiles.

Secretly, Hurst agreed with the magician's observation, to which he could personally testify: his friend liked nothing more than to have an audience hanging on his every word. But he had to admit that he did it with flair. With a mischievous gleam in his eye, the detective continued:

"As recently as last night, my friend Hurst pointed out that this business seemed to be bedeviled by animals. And, my goodness, how true that was, in so many ways. We had spoken of chicken, cats and sardines, not to mention red herrings. But there was one even more relevant: the wild goose! For we have been chasing that creature from the moment we found the tin, and automatically assumed Soudard's message referred to it: 'The cat brought a tin'. But the phone lines into the superintendent's office are rather indistinct, and what Soudard actually said was something else."

Charles clapped his hand to his forehead:

"I've got it. Soudard actually said 'The cat brought it in'!"

"Yes," said Twist, "speaking, of course about the poison. I think we would have realised that straight away, had we not happened to find a tin of sardines and set off with such enthusiasm on a wild goose chase."

"But I still don't see," interrupted Faux with some irritation, "how a cat could have brought in the cyanide."

Twist smiled and turned suddenly in the direction of the window, his ears pricking up. There was the sound of foliage being shaken, and then a sleek shape appeared framed in the window. It was a stray cat with mottled fur, and it seemed as surprised as the humans. It mewed quietly, as if to question why they were there and then, noticing Doctor Manant standing at the back of the room, it jumped down and went across to him, rubbing itself against his legs while purring contentedly. The young doctor turned as red as a beetroot. Sensing the enquiring eyes of his colleagues on him, he stuttered:

"Here, pussy, pussy. It's Michel Soudard's cat. A very affectionate animal, as you can see."

"Yes, Manant, we can see that only too well, alas!" said the professor, looking at the young doctor with reproachful eyes. Then, turning to the magician he said:

"So, Monsieur Faux, expert in criminal science, has the cat got your tongue?"

Faux was silent for a moment, then exclaimed:

"Hell's bell's! I think I've got it!"

Twist nodded his head and approached Manant:

"Your affection for cats is what betrayed you, doctor. I suppose you either gave him an antidote, or washed him thoroughly afterwards. But it
doesn't matter either way. In any case, it was very devious on your part to
direct us towards the book as part of the solution. I imagine that your plan
was to implicate Philippe Faux in the crime?"

A wild look suddenly came into Manant's eyes, which were locked on
the magician. In a voice trembling with emotion, he stammered:

"Yes, and I cannot find words to describe the conduct of this despicable
individual, who was once my friend. There is nothing he would not do out
of greed, even walk on the graves of the dead. I was personally involved
in the death of a poor woman who took her own life because she couldn't
continue to pay for his so-called services and couldn't bring herself to tell
her husband that she had spent all their money. And my colleagues can tell
similar stories. The fellow has much to answer for and many tragedies on
his conscience."

"If the justice of man fails, Dr. Manant," replied Twist, "don't forget
there is another, higher form."

"In that case, I pray with all my heart that it will swiftly complete what
I started."

"And for which you didn't hesitate to kill Soudard, if I'm correct?"

Manant shrugged his shoulders:

"I had some angry words with him recently, about a loan which he was
pressing me to repay. But he hated Philippe Faux, too. I'm sure that, in his
own way, he would have appreciated his sacrifice. He had cancer of the kid-
ney and refused to be treated. He would have been condemned to a life of
suffering anyway. I just saved him all that pain."

"It was you, then, who sent him 'Death Had Wings'?"

"Yes, it was a book he had been trying to find for some time, as I already
told you. I guessed that as soon as he got it, he would start to read it. But, if
you had been doing your job properly as policemen, you would have found
this bastard's fingerprints on the package. I managed to get him to touch it
without him being aware of what he was doing."

"We found them this morning," confirmed the superintendent, "but
Professor Twist specifically requested that I withhold that information until our little meeting."

Alan Twist nodded in agreement, then asked:

"I assume that you put your plan on hold after Faux threatened Soudard?"

"Yes, but I only put the finishing touches in place in the last few days, after I phoned Soudard to ask after his health. He told me he had caught the 'flu."

"Which was highly convenient because it allowed you to use a particularly subtle ruse. A ruse which was practically certain to succeed, and which didn't actually depend on which book the victim chose, did it?"

Vincent Manant nodded in acknowledgement then, swallowing hard, asked:

"How . . . how did you work it out?"

"It just so happens that I, too, like cats (unlike my friend Hurst, who doesn't even care to touch them). It occurred to me yesterday evening as I was letting my little friend into the house. I remembered that Soudard had the habit of stroking his cat and moistening his fingers as he read. It would have been better for him that day if he had been more careful when the affectionate little creature climbed up the wisteria, just as it did today. All you had to do to commit the perfect crime was to coat its backbone with cyanide. The cat, in a manner of speaking, got Soudard's tongue."

THE NIGHT OF THE WOLF

"Daddy, Daddy, tell us a story."

The chieftain looked at the little group that was devouring with gusto the deer that had been killed a few hours before. He pricked up his ears and glanced in exasperation at his son.

"Yes, Daddy, please," insisted another of his children.

"Another one," he growled. "You'd do better to occupy yourselves with more important things! You're old enough to hunt now. The winter's been hard and spring is still a long way off. How many times do I have to tell you that to live you have to eat, and to eat you have-"

"Yes, we know, but please Daddy, please tell—"

"Now you're bothering me! I don't know what else to tell!"

His companion trotted through the snow to rub herself against him:

"You can tell them the story of Wolf."

"The story of Wolf!" he bristled. "But they're much too young."

"Yes, tell us the story," his turbulent offspring clamoured in unison.

He bared his teeth in anger, but he soon relented; he knew that, one way or another, he would not be able to escape the daily chore. After all, if they were old enough to hunt, they were old enough to know.

He gazed for a long time at the plain covered in snow and, in the distance, the dark line of the pine trees bowing to the wind. With his red eyes fixed on his sons, he began:

"It's a very sad story. Most among us claim that 'those things' only exist in the minds of a few crazy creatures. Unfortunately, it's not true. Wolf was a friend . . . . "

The snow was falling in thick flakes on Eastmorland. It was only eight o'clock in the evening, but the inhabitants of that small village in the north of England had already double-bolted their doors. Terror, rather than the rigours of winter, was what chilled their hearts. Only two days had gone by since the murder of old Peter Wolf. A particularly grisly murder, yet –curiously- it was not so much the ferocity of the crime which worried the villagers, but what it implied. "*He* is back," they could be heard whispering. "My God, what will become of us? Our women? Our children?"

Chief Inspector John Reilly, in charge of the investigation, had hardly slept since the tragedy. That evening, he was pacing up and down in front of the fireplace, racking his brains for any glimmer of a solution to the extraordinary puzzle, when someone knocked on the door.

He went to open it. An old man of smallish stature stood there, covered in snow and obviously numb with cold, claiming to be lost and looking for an inn in which to spend the night. A short while later, sitting in front of the fire with a stiff grog, he explained to his host the circumstances which had led him to lose his way. Totally preoccupied, the policeman only listened with one ear. One phrase, however, caught his attention:

" . . . There's always an explanation for everything."

John Reilly studied the visitor carefully. His gnarled and twisted hands and his face like parchment spoke to a great number of years on this earth. His eyes, by contrast, were striking for their sparkling vitality, youth, and intelligence. Reilly was unsure what to make of him. Where had this old man come from anyway? Why had he been wandering out in the open at this time of night, in the swirling snow? His clothes appeared to be of good quality; there was nothing of the tramp about him. The detective began to regret not having paid enough attention to what he had been saying. But good manners prevented him from asking his companion to repeat his words.

"For everything? Do you really believe that?" he remarked, with a disillusioned smile. "Mr.—Mr.—?"

"Farrell. Irving Farrell. Yes, I believe there *is* always an explanation for everything."

John Reilly shook his head disapprovingly as he stared at the wolfhound sleeping on one corner of the carpet. Mr. Farrell frowned.

"Would there be a connection between that animal and your reluctance to believe?"

"Yes, in a way. I took in this hound because his master was murdered nearly two days ago. And, speaking of explanations, there isn't one for the death of that man. No 'rational' one, at least. It has been proven that only this beast could have been responsible, but it's beyond the bounds of credibility that it could have administered the fatal dagger wound."

"The animal looks harmless enough to me, in spite of its size," Mr. Farrell observed calmly.

"I think so too, even though the body of his master, Mr. Wolf, had been lacerated by claw marks and fang marks."

The old man looked at him, wide-eyed.

"Stabbed, bitten, and slashed? What kind of a monster . . . . "

"Have you ever heard tell of the *werewolf*, my dear sir?" asked the policeman.

The visitor looked at him incredulously.

"There's always an explanation for everything, you say," John Reilly continued bitterly, and with a note of sarcasm. "I think you'll change your mind after I've told you what happened the night before last, as well as certain events which occurred about twenty years ago. One of the two people who discovered the victim is none other than my predecessor, ex-Chief Inspector Maurice Wildfire. A level-headed witness, in other words, with a trained eye.

"It had snowed that night, between nine o'clock and midnight. It was a little after that when Wildfire was awakened by screams and growls. Around one o'clock there was a knock at the door. It was his old friend and neighbour Dr. Lessing, standing there with a torch in one hand and his walking-stick in the other, who asked him whether he had heard screams coming from the forest. Anxiously, and for good reason, they went straight away to Peter Wolf's house.

"Wildfire and Lessing both lived practically at the edge of the forest. They only had to follow a path through the woods to reach Wolf's house, which was situated in the middle of a clearing. A house made entirely of wood, with a carpenter's workshop adjoining, although Wolf had not set foot there for several years, having given up his hobby.

"It was not long after one o'clock that Dr. Lessing and Wildfire reached the clearing. A thin coat of fresh snow covered the frozen ground all around. The beam of Dr. Lessing's lamp picked out a strange set of prints which appeared to originate in the Wolf house, standing about fifty yards ahead of them. They were not the footprints of a human, but of a large dog—or a wolf!

"The prints petered out quite close to them, not far from the path and almost indistinguishable under the trees and bushes. In the light of the lamp they traced the prints back, which led them to the front entrance of Wolf's house, open in that weather and at that late hour! They found Wolf slumped in front of the fireplace, swimming in his own blood, a dagger planted in his back and his face and limbs lacerated with slashes. The body was still warm. Dr. Lessing estimated that death had occurred within the half hour, forty minutes at most, which placed it at about twelve thirty. An assessment confirmed later by the medical examiner. Do you see the problem? The crime occurred *after* the snow stopped. Now, apart from their own and those of the 'beast', no other footprints were found anywhere around the house—which they searched from top to bottom, only to prove that nobody was there, other than themselves and the victim. Even the victim's wretched dog had disappeared. They were probably its prints that they had noticed outside and, while it may have been responsible for the vicious attack on its master, under no circumstances could it have stabbed him with a dagger. How, then, had the murderer escaped without leaving a mark in the snow?"

Mr. Farrell nodded his head, deep in thought. He drained his grog, savouring the last drop, then declared:

"Interesting. But how much time had elapsed before your arrival on the scene?"

Chief Inspector Reilly smiled ironically as he answered:

"I understand what's behind your question. Actually, we got there very quickly. Dr. Lessing came immediately to find me, leaving Wildfire to stay with the victim. It's the business about the footprints that intrigues you, isn't it? I can assure you that was where we focussed our attention, because Dr. Lessing had pointed out their curious nature straight away. It just so happened that among my officers there was a specialist in that area, who knows more than an Apache Indian about the tricks that can be played. None of the sets of tracks had been tampered with. Not those of the 'beast', not Wildfire's, not Dr. Lessing's. Nobody had marched backwards, nobody had covered anyone else's prints with his own. And I repeat, there were no other prints around the house, nor anywhere on the snow-covered surface of the clearing. We also went through Wildfire's house with a fine-toothed comb. Nothing, and—needless to say—no secret passages. Are you beginning to get the picture?"

"It certainly limits the possibilities. What did the medical examiner have to say about the wounds?"

"He was fairly cautious. Wolf's face and hands had been shredded, not bitten; in fact there were no clear bite marks anywhere. It was the work of a wild animal, there's nothing more to be said. As for the dagger wound in the back, that was without question the work of a human. A precise blow, straight to the heart, causing instantaneous death."

Mr. Farrell thought for a moment, then pointed to the wolfhound sleeping on the carpet:

"When and where did you find him?"

"He reappeared during the morning. We examined him carefully, of course. He seemed to have been in a fight, but there was nothing to show whether it had been with his master or another animal in the area. The problem is there had been another fall of snow since the night, so we couldn't compare his prints to those leaving the front entrance of the house."

"But those prints must have been made by the dog, surely?"

"Perhaps. But in that case, what about the murderer? A winged assassin, not subject to the laws of gravity, do you think? Whether it was this beast or some other animal that shredded his master's body, doesn't affect the problem, as I see it! How could whoever had struck the fatal blow have escaped? By the way, this dog doesn't strike me as being particularly aggressive . . . Otherwise, believe me, I wouldn't be keeping him here".

There was a silence, broken by Mr. Farrell asking:

"Apart from what you've told me, are there any other clues?"

"Clues? No. There was something bizarre, however, although I can't see what it could have to do with the murder. On the bench in the workshop there were some fresh wood shavings, which apparently had come from a lath from the roof which we found on one of the shelves, the only bit of freshly cut wood in a place covered with dust and cobwebs."

"That's certainly bizarre. But what's even more bizarre is the conclusion you seem to have drawn from all this. If I've understood you correctly, you think Mr. Wolf's killer was half-man, half-wolf, in other words a werewolf, which would explain the claw marks and the bites, as well as the dagger and the prints in the snow."

John Reilly nodded, somewhat shamefacedly.

"I assume, my dear sir, that you must have good reasons for making such an assumption?"

The chief inspector's face darkened and his voice dropped.

"You're not from these parts, I take it? You don't know about the legend which hangs over this village. The werewolf has always haunted this region. A monster, half-man half-wolf, as you say, which has its own particular way of killing its prey: tearing the flesh apart with its fangs before plunging a dagger into the heart. About twenty years ago, nothing had been heard of the werewolf for some time. Then, out of the blue, it struck twice. Old Timothy saw it with his own eyes when it attacked Henry, the little boy he had adopted and who, by some miracle, survived. The old man's dog, like his master, tried to defend the child against the monster and followed it into the forest, where it was found in agony, its body lacerated by dagger thrusts. Incidentally, the tragedy was seen by another witness, none other than Dr. Lessing, whose own wife would be a victim of the 'beast' a week later."

For a few seconds, the only sound to be heard was the crackling of the fire. The two men stared sightlessly at the sleeping wolfhound. The smooth and shiny fur of its flank rose and fell steadily with the rhythm of its breathing.

It was Reilly that broke the silence:

"Have you any *other* explanation to offer, my dear sir?"

The old man avoided the question.

"You told me that Mr. Wildfire and Dr. Lessing went to Mr. Wolf's house because they had reason to be concerned. I don't really understand that. Admittedly they both heard growls coming from the forest, but that was hardly reason enough for a nocturnal excursion. Especially since the werewolf had not been seen for about twenty years!"

"Obviously," replied John Reilly, turning his armchair around. "It wasn't only the noises that caused them to be concerned about old Wolf. Several days before the tragedy, Wildfire and Lessing had spent the evening with him. Henry was there, too. Yes, the very same Henry who had been attacked by the 'beast' in the past. This kind of get-together was unusual, quite exceptional in fact, because Wolf had lived practically as a recluse since he had stopped working. I say since that time, because before then he had been a busy bee, dipping into every flower. He was an unrepentant skirt-chaser, to the point that he had no friends left among the males of the village. A state of affairs which had made him bitter and even hateful. Although surprised by the invitation, Wildfire and Lessing accepted, assuming that the hermit's life was beginning to weigh on him. And that night, the discussion turned to the werewolf."

Reilly stopped and looked his visitor in the eye to get his full attention:

"I imagine you are well aware that the werewolf is a human of normal appearance, male or female, who only turns into a wild beast during certain nights. Are they complete transformations? Are they partial? Are they frequent? Do they only happen at full moon? I'm not going to dwell on the subject, which is in any case very controversial, as is the way to combat them: only silver bullets that have been blessed and marked with the cross are supposed to be effective. The question of the 'transmission' of the evil is of particular importance, in my opinion. Some believe that a simple bite is sufficient to give birth to a 'new wolf'.

"Then there's also the question of what symptoms allow us to identify our werewolf when he is not in a period of transformation. They say that, despite the human appearance, two things can betray him. First, his body will show the marks of any wounds and any scratches sustained during his wild wanderings in the forest. Second, there will be hairs on the palm of his hand. Wildfire, Lessing, and Wolf were discussing the matter when the conversation became quite heated. It was about Henry, in fact, who had actually been bitten by the monster, and who had suffered the consequences.

"He's a good and honest lad, but he has the mental age of an eight year old. In the village, he is called upon to perform only the most menial tasks, which often involve cuts and scratches. He has no hairs on his palm, but his body and arms are covered in a veritable fleece. It's not difficult to guess the drift of the discussion: Henry, having been bitten by the monster, must surely run the risk of becoming a werewolf one day. Wildfire and Lessing pressed the point and that, apparently, riled Wolf. He suddenly announced, with a sneer, that the time had come to tell Henry the 'truth'; and not just Henry but the whole village.

"What truth was he talking about? The doctor and the ex-policeman failed to get it out of him, but they formed the distinct impression that Wolf was intent on pouring derision on the werewolf legend. They pointed out that his attitude might cause him grief if the werewolf got wind of what he was saying. Whereupon there was a minor incident: Dr. Lessing made a sudden movement; the dog had an unfortunate reaction and bit him in the ankle. Nothing serious, but afterwards Lessing had been obliged to walk with a cane for a few days. From that moment, things went from bad to worse, not helped by the amount of alcohol that had been consumed. Wildfire and Lessing left, threatening the old man with another visit from the monster, in view of his cynical disdain. Wolf, sarcastic and sneering, kept repeating that everyone would soon learn the truth."

Once more, Mr. Farrell nodded his head approvingly in amusement and satisfaction.

"Very well," he said after a while. "So we're dealing with a werewolf. A werewolf that visited Mr. Wolf by night and killed him with bites and a blow from a dagger, before exiting the house, leaving behind his footprints in the virgin snow. All we need to do is to find his identity, the human face behind which he is hiding. Have you an idea? Any suspects? Personally, I would lean towards one of the three people with him that night. And you?"

John Reilly cleared his throat.

"Yes, I'm also suspicious of those three. Particularly since none of them has an alibi. At the time of the crime, in other words around twelve thirty, Wildfire and Lessing were both at home alone, and Henry was sleeping it off in a barn after an anniversary dinner for the farmer who employs him. Regarding Henry, I think I should tell you that all of Wolf's estate comes to him, so he inherits the house and any savings the old man had. Did Wildfire and Lessing have a similar motive for murder? I don't know. But I've always suspected that Wildfire held a grudge against Wolf: it appears that his wife left him shortly after they came to live here. Could it be that she had an affair with Wolf and then, full of remorse, left the scene? All that is pure speculation, of course. And, as for Dr. Lessing, all we have is conjecture. The doctor remarried after the tragic disappearance of his first wife. A happy and tranquil union, apparently, marred only by the poor state of health of the new Mrs. Lessing, who left us several years ago. Since then, he has lived alone, his only company a young dog, much sought after by the animal that you see lying in front you."

Reilly's voice trailed off, surprised as he was by the sudden change in the old man's expression, which had gone from a deep frown to a broad smile. He turned towards the policeman:

"We're looking for a monster and you talk to me about motives for murder? I have the impression that you are not as convinced as you would have me believe in the existence of this famous werewolf. Mr. Reilly, I believe that, deep down, you have never really believed in the legend. And I still maintain there's always an explanation for everything."

"Am I to understand from what you say that you have solved the mystery? That you are in a position to explain how a 'human' can cross an expanse of snow without leaving behind any trace other than that of an animal?"

"Yes," replied Mr. Farrell simply.

There was an icy silence.

"It's impossible," spluttered the chief inspector. "I've studied the problem from every angle and—"

"Don't forget the wood shavings."

"*The wood shavings!* What the devil can they have to do with it? And the werewolf that attacked Henry nearly twenty five years ago. Two witnesses saw it. How do you explain that?"

"The facts, Mr. Reilly, just consider the facts. Try for a moment to empty your mind and reconstruct the scene from what is known: a young boy is found with serious bite wounds, and nearby is a dog writhing in agony from knife cuts. Who bit the young boy? The dog, clearly. And who took it on himself to stab the dog to death? The adult who was there at the scene, obviously, who wanted to put down the crazed animal who had attacked his adopted son.

"Old Timothy must have thought for a moment that little Henry was dead; that he hadn't been able to save him; and that he might even have struck him during his ferocious attack on his own dog. Beside himself with grief, weighed down by a sense of guilt, he felt he was losing his reason. It's not surprising that he regarded his dog as a sort of monster, nor that he started talking about the terrible 'beast' of the legend.

"Once you accept that as the starting point, it's child's play to work out what happened next. I can only see one explanation for the lie that Dr. Lessing told. As witness to the tragedy, he confirmed the old man's ramblings in order to be able to blame the werewolf for a crime that he had been planning for some time: disposing of his wife, who had deceived him with Wolf. The affair is pure speculation on my part, he may well have killed his first wife for some other reason. I also have the feeling that Henry is the fruit of another one of Wolf's amorous adventures.

"If we make that assumption, it explains a lot of what happened. If Wolf had been Mrs. Lessing's lover, he could well suspect that her death was actually a murder motivated by jealousy and that, in the shadow of the wild werewolf, there lurked the good doctor. If Wolf was the father of Henry, that would explain why he left him his estate and why he did not appreciate, at that notorious dinner, Wildfire and Lessing's assumption that Henry could be—or become—a werewolf. It must have been even more galling for him in view of what he suspected about Lessing. No prizes for guessing why the doctor continued to foster the legend twenty years after. Wolf flew into a rage and let Dr. Lessing know that he had discovered his secret and did not intend to keep quiet about it much longer, not realising that, in doing so, he was signing his own death warrant.

"In order to get rid of Wolf without attracting suspicion, Dr. Lessing needed to make it look like a new manifestation of the werewolf. So the following day, even though the wound inflicted by Wolf's dog was minor, he started walking with a cane. And a few days later, when a light snowfall was anticipated, he put his plan into action. That evening as the snow started to fall, he walked to the clearing, taking with him his young dog, which he attached to a tree. He knocked on Wolf's door. He stabbed him and lacerated his skin with the same special tool he had used on his first wife some twenty years earlier. Then he went into the disused carpenter's workshop and fashioned a rudimentary pair of stilts from the roof lath, shaping the tips so that they matched the end of his cane. Or possibly he made them some time before, even in the presence of Wolf, who was completely oblivious to the intended purpose of the stilts.

"The snow having stopped, the killer unleashed his dog and watched it hurtle towards the edge of the forest to meet its mate in joyful reunion— which was the cause of the noise that became 'shrieks and growls' in Lessing's words. In turn, the doctor himself left the scene on the stilts. Of course, these were not full size stilts, which would have left widely spaced marks; in this case, the chocks which supported the feet were nailed close to the base of the stilts—in other words only a few inches from the ground—which would result in a very short stride and hence closely spaced marks in an almost straight line, similar to those made by a cane. After having released his dog, he alerted the ex-Chief Inspector Wildfire. Then, arriving on the scene in the company of his friend, he immediately shone his light on the dog's prints, while walking next to those left by the stilts, and pretending to press down on his cane.

"The policeman in charge of examining the prints did his job very thoroughly, I have no doubt. I'm sure he carefully examined all the prints left in the snow by Wildfire, Lessing, and the dog. But the marks left by the cane?"

The chief inspector's ears were ringing and his brain was in a swirling fog. He could not believe it. This providential visitor had solved, in less than a quarter of an hour, a puzzle he had been racking his brains over for two days and almost two nights. He could only hear the voice off and on, in snatches:

"The fresh wood shavings were quite clear, after all . . . I kept telling you there's always an explanation for everything . . . Look! It's stopped snowing! I'll be on my way soon . . . No, doggie, down . . . Stay . . . You're staying here . . . What's his name by the way?"

"Wolf," murmured Reilly, "like his deceased master. I never understood why he called him by his own name."

"There's always an explanation for everything, my dear sir . . . . "

Night started to fall. A few flakes of snow swirled in the biting cold. Nothing remained of the deer except the carcass lying in a pool of blood-red melted snow. Still, some of the group were not yet sated, but continued to feast on the last scraps of flesh, tearing at them with unabated ferocity.

"You understand," said the chief as he concluded the story, "that it was not the right solution."

"Personally," growled his eldest son, "I find the story grotesque. Particularly the bit about being transformed into half-man half-wolf."

"Unfortunately, my son, it happens. But in the opposite sense, naturally. That was precisely the case with Wolf. Because it was he, of course, who killed the old man during one of his many fits. I have, as it happens, seen one of them. You cannot imagine anything more hideous! He lost his beautiful fur

and his paws lengthened and spread apart. His heavy furless head became round, his ears shrank and his snout—I don't even want to think about it—almost disappeared. Truly a monster. But that's enough for tonight. We have to break camp."

A long howl rent the silence. At the chief's call, those who were still feasting withdrew their blooded snouts from the deer's entrails. And the pack disappeared into the depths of the forest.

ACKNOWLEDGEMENTS

We—and Paul—are greatly indebted to the following people:

Jon Breen, noted reviewer and doyen of mystery fiction critics,
for his vigorous encouragement;

Barry Ergang, Managing Editor of *Futures Mystery Anthology Magazine*,
for his early encouragement and counsel;

Ed Hoch, prolific writer of short stories and himself an acknowledged
master of the impossible crime, for his advocacy;

Janet Hutchings, editor of *Ellery Queen's Mystery Magazine*,
for giving Paul the chance to finally display his wares for an English
speaking audience;

Roland Lacourbe, both for introducing this book
and for introducing us to Paul;

Brian Skupin, co-publisher of *Mystery Scene*, for his invaluable advice.

We hope that we have not overlooked anyone,
but apologise in advance if that is the case.

BIOGRAPHIES

Paul Halter was born in Hagenau, Alsace, in 1956. After serving in the French Marines, he tried his hand selling life insurance and playing the guitar in night-clubs. In 1987 he carried off the top prize at the prestigious Festival of Cognac for detective fiction with *La Quatrieme Porte* (*The Fourth Door*), and in the following year received one of the highest accolades in French mystery literature, the Prix du Roman d'Aventures, for *Le Brouillard Rouge* (*The Red Fog*), joining the company of such exalted writers as Pierre Boileau and Thomas Narcejac. To date, he has written thirty novels, all but two of which feature seemingly impossible crimes, and has become one of France's best-selling mystery authors. Three of his short stories have appeared in *EQMM*.

Roland Lacourbe is the noted French authority on 'locked-room' fiction: author of "John Dickson Carr, Scribe du Miracle," "99 Chambres Closes," and "Houdini et Sa Legende"; and editor of numerous locked-room anthologies. His early advocacy of Paul Halter's work contributed to its initial success and he was responsible for the introduction to the original short story collection.

Bob Adey has enjoyed reading detective fiction ever since he stumbled across it as an impressionable teenager. Stories of impossible crime have always been one of his particular fascinations and in 1979 he published a bibliography on the subject: "Locked Room Murders," which was revised and enlarged in 1991. He has also over the years, often in collaboration with like minded enthusiasts, been responsible for several locked room anthologies and has edited or contributed to numerous collections. But it is probably for his impossible crime bibliography that he is best known.

John Pugmire has been an avid amateur enthusiast of 'locked-room' stories for many years, and an admirer of Paul Halter's work since it first appeared. He has authored articles about M. Halter's work and impossible crimes in general. In addition to being co-translator with Bob Adey, he is responsible for the liberal adaptation of M. Lacourbe's original introduction.